Praise for

Neo's Realm

The sexy tale delves into the emotional journey Gunnar is forced to take, as well as Ramiro's reflection on his own past... Crimson Moon fulfills its potential as the hot, entertaining tale it is. ~ *Joyfully Reviewed*

...incredible story...I love how each book builds on the previous one in the series adding to the thrill and suspense... ~ *Fallen Angels Reviews*

...full of twists that help move the series forward...an excellent addition to the Neo's Realm series...
 ~ *Literary Nymphs Reviews*

You will feel as if you are there with the characters taking a stroll through the woods, or camping out waiting for the enemy... This story is truly one of inspiration ~ *Whipped Cream Reviews*

...captures the imagination and snags the reader from page one...an excellent piece of literature...this definitely left me wanting more
~ *Ecata Sensual Reviews*

Rawley's Redemption
Twin Temptations
It's a Good Life

Cattle Valley Volume One
All Play & No Work
Cattle Valley Mistletoe

Cattle Valley Volume Two
Sweet Topping
Rough Ride

Cattle Valley Volume Three
Physical Therapy
Out of the Shadow

Cattle Valley Volume Four
Bad Boy Cowboy
The Sound of White

Cattle Valley Volume Five
Gone Surfin'
The Last Bouquet

Cattle Valley Volume Six
Eye of the Beholder
Cattle Valley Days

Cattle Valley Volume Seven
Bent— Not Broken
Arm Candy

Cattle Valley Volume Eight
Recipe for Love
Firehouse Heat

Cattle Valley Volume Nine
Neil's Guardian Angel
Scarred

NEO'S REALM
Volume Two

Crimson Moon

Royal Blood

CAROL LYNNE

Neo's Realm Volume Two
ISBN # 978-1-78184-659-9
©Copyright Carol Lynne 2013
Cover Art by April Martinez ©Copyright 2013
Interior text design by Claire Siemaszkiewicz
Totally Bound Publishing

Published in 2013 by Totally Bound Publishing, Newland House, The Point, Weaver Road, Lincoln, LN6 3QN, United Kingdom.

Totally Bound Publishing is an imprint of Total-E-Ntwined Limited.

CRIMSON MOON

Dedication

A special thanks to Jambrea and Theresa A.

Chapter One

His nose buried in a book, Ramiro Delgado lazily rested his hand on the blond head of the fae who was currently sucking him off under the table. *The Frenzy*, the neighbourhood feeding bar in The Realm, only had a few patrons this early in the evening, and Ramiro planned to take advantage of the calm before the rush.

The tongue flicking the head of his cock was delightful, but when Ramiro felt the fae trying to work magic by probing his hole, Ramiro grunted. "Stick to the cock, kid."

Kid? Ramiro shoved away that particular image. The little fae under the table was probably twice his age. There was just something about the spritely-looking fae that made him think of them as younger.

When the fae's tongue drilled its way into the slit on Ramiro's crown, he'd had enough of the game. Fisting the fae's curls, Ramiro plunged his entire length down the creature's throat and came. The climax wasn't satisfying and wouldn't sustain his desire for long, but at least he could go where he needed without showing his desire for the one he couldn't have.

Ramiro waited until he heard the fae cry his own orgasm before pushing his chair back. He stood and stuffed his softened cock back into his suit pants. "Thanks." He took the time to brush his palm over the fae's cheek before picking up his book and heading out of the door.

As he walked towards the palace, Ramiro's thoughts went to the book in his hand. It was an ancient diary-of-sorts that he'd found in The Realm's archives. It was more-or-less an instruction manual, full of ideas on how to retain humanity after being turned.

Although Ramiro was supposed to be looking for ways to defeat the hybrid creatures Morwyn had created, it had given him an idea. He stepped up to the gate surrounding the palace Ian Kildare had created, and waited. Because of the strong wards surrounding the palace, there was no need for a guard at the gate. Only those imbued with the proper clearance could enter without instant evaporation. With so many magical creatures living in The Realm, other forms of identity clearance just weren't feasible.

Ramiro entered the King of the Vampire's palace with purpose. "Where's the King?" he asked one of the guards under his command.

"Dining room," the guard answered without making eye contact.

When he reached his destination, Ramiro stopped at the closed doors. "When you have a moment," he called through the heavily carved wood.

From within, a cry of release sounded. "Enter," Ian ordered.

Ramiro opened the door just as Ian pulled his robe closed. The human on the table in front of him was naked, as usual, with a sated smile on his face. The quickly-healing holes on the human's neck told Ramiro, without words, the King had just fed from the man.

Holding up the book, Ramiro approached the head of the table. "I was wondering if I may speak to you about something I've just read?"

"Of course." Ian settled himself back into his chair. "I see you've found my diary. I must've been mad to give that over to the archives, but I was young and stupid at the time." Ian claimed to be the first vampire, Faelan, the mysterious King of the Fae had created. Because no one had ever stepped up to contest his claim, Ramiro believed him.

Ramiro took a seat close to Ian. The two of them had become close friends over the years, and although he showed Ian the utmost respect in front of others, when it was just the two of them he could cut out the formalities and talk to Ian as a friend. He glanced at the Royal Donor on the table. Ian was the only vampire in The Realm allowed human donors, and the smell of the human's blood called to Ramiro. He swallowed the saliva pooling in his mouth and tried to concentrate on the reason he'd sought Ian's expertise.

Ian chuckled and reached out to caress the inner thigh of his donor. "Would you like something to eat?"

Yes, Ramiro wanted to scream, but he knew it was forbidden. It was punishable by death for any vampire to drink from one of the Royal Donors. "Thank you, but I've already eaten once this evening."

Again, Ramiro tried to get his thoughts on track, while Ian continued to stroke the man in front of him. "I seek your advice, old friend."

"Then you shall have it," Ian answered.

"You write about ways to preserve humanity for those turned. It has me wondering whether it would be possible to preserve your wolf if a shifter was turned."

Ian released his hold on the donor's cock. "Leave us," he told the hardening man.

"Yes, Your Majesty." The donor rose before donning the sheer red robe of his station.

Ian waited for the man to leave before returning his attention to Ramiro. "I gather this is about your friend…"

"Gunnar," Ramiro supplied with a roll of his eyes. Not only had Ramiro spoken to Ian of Gunnar, but the King had met the Alpha werewolf before the kidnapping and subsequent changing of the wolf.

"Yes, Gunnar." There was a devilish grin on Ian's face as he rested his entwined fingers on his chest. "I've never heard of a vampire retaining his animal traits once turned, but then there are so few."

"But do you think it's possible?" Ramiro prompted.

"Possible? Probably. But I'd strongly caution against the attempt. It's different when humans are turned because they're weak. Their human selves will step back and allow the vampire side of them to take the lead. I don't see that happening with a were, especially an Alpha. The result could easily be insanity along with the inability to stay in one form."

Ramiro nodded. Everything Ian said made sense, but he still wanted to tell Gunnar there was a chance of holding onto his wolf. The further Gunnar's wolf slipped away, the harder it became for the Alpha. Ramiro hated to admit it, but he missed the posturing the two of them had once engaged in.

"You're going to try it anyway," Ian surmised.

"I'm going to tell Gunnar there's a chance, and let him make up his own mind."

The grin was back on Ian's handsome face. "You love him."

"I do not." Ramiro stood. "I just hate to see a strong man weakened."

"If you say so." Ian rang the small brass bell in front of him. A voluptuous woman stepped into the room wearing a sheer red robe. "If you'll excuse me. I think it's time for dessert."

Ramiro bowed his head before exiting the dining room, leaving the book on the table. It was one thing to watch Ian play with a handsome man, but he'd never felt desire for a woman's body. He left the palace in search of Gunnar.

* * * *

Gunnar shifted his weight on the uncomfortable cement bench. Although the park was the one place in all The Realm that felt like home, the benches were pure torture. He supposed it was to assure no lingering, but it would be nice to be able to at least sit for a couple of hours and enjoy the trees and grass.

With that thought in mind, Gunnar stood and stepped over the small rock wall onto the plush green grass. Although there were signs posted to stay on the paths, Gunnar didn't care. He needed to feel the earth under him. His wolf might be dying, but it still called out to him from deep inside.

"Breaking the law? I'm surprised at you," Ramiro said from the sidewalk.

Gunnar didn't bother opening his eyes. "Arrest me. Send me back to Italy." He held up his hands, wrists together. "Got cuffs?"

Ramiro chuckled, the deep sound of his voice going straight to Gunnar's cock. *Fuck!* Gunnar hated the attraction he felt for the vampire. Before he'd been turned, Gunnar had been able to appreciate Ramiro's masculine sex appeal, but that was as far as it went. However, the more he tried to accept his new life, the more his body responded to the centuries-old vampire.

Gunnar sat up in hopes of hiding his erection. "Did you want something?"

Ramiro stepped over the barricade and stared down at Gunnar, hands in the pockets of his black designer suit pants. "Why are you wallowing on the ground?" he asked in apparent disgust.

"Because it feels good." Gunnar ran his fingers through the thick green carpet of grass. "If you weren't such a sissy, you'd get down here and join me." *Shit.* Why the hell had he said that? Gunnar felt like biting off his own tongue.

Instead of sitting in the grass, Ramiro squatted down. The new position gave Gunnar an even better look at the large cock trapped behind the thin suit pants. "I need to talk to you about something, but I'm not about to sit on wet grass in order to do it. Why don't we go down the street and get a drink?"

Gunnar averted his gaze. "It's not wet yet. You think I'm stupid?"

"Whatever." Ramiro ducked his head enough to stare into Gunnar's eyes. "Come on, have a drink with me."

The last thing in the world Gunnar wanted was to accompany Ramiro to The Frenzy. He'd been talked into it once before and hadn't been able to look at Ramiro in the same way since. It wasn't the feeding that bothered him. It was watching the little fae fuckers service Ramiro right in front of him.

"I'm not going to The Frenzy again. I've already told you that."

"Wasn't talking about going there. Besides, I've already eaten this evening." Ramiro stood and held out his hand. "I thought a nice glass of Liquid Crimson at Giovanni's would be nice."

Gunnar slapped Ramiro's hand out of his way and stood. With his feet back under him, Gunnar discreetly adjusted his hardening cock before stepping back onto the cement path. Trying to get his mind off his body's desires, he decided to make small talk as they walked side by side towards the bar.

"Why don't they want us on the grass?"

Ramiro glanced at Gunnar before returning his attention to the sidewalk in front of them. "Because, as you've already discovered, it calls to your were instincts." He cleared his throat, suddenly looking extremely uncomfortable. "After being here for so long, the other weres wouldn't be able to control their shift, and The Realm isn't equipped for hunting."

"And by other weres, I take it you mean everyone but me," Gunnar surmised. Gods, if only he could still shift, but they both knew it wasn't even a possibility.

"Maybe," Ramiro mumbled.

"What's that supposed to mean?"

Ramiro opened the door to the bar and motioned Gunnar inside. Gunnar had only been to Giovanni's on a few occasions, but he found he liked the dark atmosphere. Maybe it was because it seemed to match his mood lately.

They found an empty half-round booth at the back along one wall. Gunnar slid in one side while Ramiro raised his hand to get the waitress's attention. He held up two fingers and the woman nodded. Ramiro sat down across the table and scooted in until his back was to the wall.

Gunnar grinned. Ramiro always seemed ready for a fight. He wondered if the vamp ever let down his guard for more than a few minutes. They both remained quiet until the waitress brought two stemmed glasses of the intoxicating wine and blood mixture. "So what did you want to talk about?" he asked after several sips.

"Does your wolf still speak to you?"

Gunnar sat back further in the booth. It was the first time in several weeks his wolf had been mentioned. Gunnar thought about his uninterrupted moments in the grass earlier. "Sometimes, but not the way it used to. Why?"

Ramiro's dark eyes narrowed. "You felt it earlier, didn't you?"

"Yes," Gunnar admitted.

"I read something earlier that has me thinking."

"Dangerous," Gunnar said, cutting Ramiro off.

"Shut up and listen," Ramiro countered. "According to the book, the best way for vampires to hold on to their humanity after being turned is by living amongst humans. It made me wonder whether we could save your wolf by having you do the things you once did as a wolf."

"I can't shift," Gunnar spat. He took a deep, calming breath. It had taken him weeks to come to terms with the changes taking place within him. Having Ramiro bring it up felt like a slap in the face.

Ramiro finished off his Liquid Crimson and signalled for two more. "I guess the bigger question is would you like to retain your wolf as part of who you are without being able to fully shift?"

The question left Gunnar speechless. How many nights had he lain awake begging the Gods to let him keep his wolf? Now, however, he wondered if keeping the wolf aware yet trapped would be even worse.

"I know it's not an easy decision to make, but you need to give it some serious thought before your wolf fades even further." Ramiro started to reach for Gunnar, but stopped and withdrew his hand, picking up the wine glass instead.

Gunnar nodded. "I will," he finally managed to say.

Ramiro's head tilted to the side. Although the movement was purely innocent, and totally Ramiro, Gunnar's body took instant notice of the candlelight reflecting in the vampire's dark eyes.

"I have to go." Gunnar pulled a wad of crumpled money from his pocket before tossing it onto the table.

Ramiro seemed surprised. His black eyebrows rose as he gestured to Gunnar's full glass of Liquid Crimson. "But you haven't finished your drink."

"Losing my head is the last thing I need right now." He slid out of the booth. "Thanks," he said before turning to dash out of the restaurant.

Once he'd made it to the sidewalk, Gunnar took off towards the park. *Fuck!* He'd been a second away from pulling Ramiro into his arms and forgetting all about his wolf. It was time to get his head on straight.

Gunnar veered from the park and headed towards the one place in all The Realm he hated most. He knew he could've asked Ramiro to accompany him to The Frenzy, but why invite hard feelings between the two of them? Gunnar hated that Ramiro fucked his way through dinner every night, but he was in no position to say anything to Ramiro about his sex life.

Standing outside the door to the packed bar, Gunnar took a deep breath. He'd only been in The Frenzy on one occasion, at Ramiro's urging. Unfortunately, as soon as he'd stepped inside the club the smell of sex and blood had nearly driven him insane. He'd wanted nothing more than to push Ramiro over a table and fuck him. No other creature in the club had appealed to him. He couldn't imagine rubbing against one of the fae. Having sex with them in exchange for their blood was absolutely out of the question as far as Gunnar was concerned, so he'd run.

Footsteps behind him drew Gunnar's attention. He glanced over his shoulder and winced at the sight of a smug-looking Ramiro walking his way.

"I would've joined you if you'd only told me you were stopping off here," Ramiro said.

"I'm not *stopping off here*. I need to speak with Audric. Since the threesome seem to spend most nights here..." Gunnar shrugged instead of finishing the sentence. "Why don't you go in and ask him to come out and talk to me?"

Ramiro crossed his arms over his chest. The gesture drew Gunnar's eyes to the muscle mass hidden under the expensive suit, weakening him further. *To give in is to give up*, he told himself once more.

"Why don't you hunger for blood the way I do?" Ramiro asked.

"Who said I didn't?" Gunnar returned defensively. "I just don't think it's worth prostituting myself to get it."

Ramiro's eyes rounded. "Is that what you think I do?"

"Isn't it? You pick up strangers to fuck in exchange for their blood. What's the difference?" Gunnar wasn't about to back down from an argument. It had become obvious Ramiro thought less of him for drinking the bottled blood The Realm provided.

Ramiro's dark eyes narrowed to mere slits as he took several steps forwards, putting himself mere inches from Gunnar's already heated body. "I'm a vampire," he stated. "You're still thinking in wolf terms. You are what you are, and the sooner you get that through that thick skull of yours, the happier your new life will be."

"So in your eyes, I need to become a slut if I want to be happy with the changes in my body that I didn't fucking ask for in the first place?" Gunnar knew he was lashing out, but he needed to do something or risk exposing his true feelings to Ramiro.

Instead of getting pissed off, Ramiro's expression softened. "Few of us had a choice in what we've become. I spent many years hating myself for desiring the one thing my body needed to survive. I'm only trying to save you from that, because your hatred won't change anything."

Gunnar swallowed around the lump in his throat at the raw emotion evident in Ramiro's voice.

Ramiro reached out and grasped Gunnar's neck, moving his thumb to brush over Gunnar's bottom lip. "I'm not a monster. The reason I give my donors what they want is to make me feel better about taking from them. I could tease them like Audric and many of the others do, but I find that...selfish."

Lost in the gentle touch, Gunnar licked the pad of Ramiro's thumb as it passed once more over his lips.

Ramiro gasped, moments before pressing his lips against Gunnar's. For several long moments, Gunnar allowed Ramiro's thrusting tongue to explore the inside of his mouth. *Gods!* For weeks he'd wondered what it would feel like to have Ramiro hold him, kiss him, fuck him. The last thought pulled Gunnar out of the haze he'd found himself in. *I'm an Alpha, damn it.*

Breaking the kiss, Gunnar pushed against Ramiro's chest. He shook his head and backed away from the tempting vampire. "I can't," he said as he turned and ran.

* * * *

Several moments later, Ramiro stood inside The Frenzy still dazed by the kiss. Damn that kiss. Why the fuck had he done something so stupid? Now that he knew Gunnar's body would respond to him, Ramiro wouldn't be able to think of anything else. He'd tried to pass his preoccupation with Gunnar off for weeks as nothing but desire, but after one kiss he knew the truth. Ian had been right, somewhere along the way he'd fallen in love with Gunnar.

"Back so soon?" the little blond fae from earlier asked.

Ramiro shook his head. "I'm looking for someone."

"I could help you," the fae offered.

Ramiro spotted Audric across the room. Although Audric was with a donor, Kern was only a few feet away. "Thanks, but I see him." He wove his way through the crowd, the taste of Gunnar still clinging to his tongue. *Fuck!* How was he supposed to concentrate on anything if he couldn't get control of his emotions?

"I need to speak with Audric," Ramiro told Kern.

Kern's gaze went to the tented pants Ramiro wore. "No."

Ramiro rolled his eyes and ran a hand over his obvious erection. "This isn't about Audric. I just need to ask him a few questions."

Kern gestured with his chin. "He's almost finished with his dinner."

Although Ramiro got along with Kern, the man was extremely protective of Audric. Ramiro knew he'd have to include Kern in the discussion if he hoped to have more than a few seconds to converse with the werewolf-turned-vampire. "Where's Haig?" Rarely did you see the three of them not together.

"With his sister," Kern answered without taking his eyes off his mate.

"Galena's here?"

"Even though she was hidden away in that fucking cage most of the time, Neo thinks she can be of some use to us. He brought her and Flick to The Realm this morning." Kern glanced up at Ramiro. "Whether or not Galena can be of help, I'm glad she's here. Haig was about to drive me crazy worrying about her."

Not having had a family for centuries, Ramiro did his best to look sympathetic. "I understand."

His poor acting job was saved by Audric's appearance. "Ready?" Audric asked Kern, cock in hand.

Kern encircled Audric's erection with his hand but shook his head. "Ramiro needs to talk to you first."

Audric's brow furrowed. "What's going on?"

Ramiro glanced around. Several sets of eyes were on them. There was no doubt the crowd waited for the nightly sex show Audric put on after feeding. "Not here."

"You're joking, right?" Audric asked, thrusting into Kern's hand.

Ramiro knew what he was asking. The sexual buzz that accompanied feeding was incredibly powerful. He decided to give Audric a break. "Meet me outside in ten minutes."

Audric nodded before climbing onto Kern's lap.

Ramiro turned away and studied the crowd. Should he indulge in a quick blow job while he waited? Gunnar's earlier statement came to mind. Although Ramiro still wasn't sure what Gunnar's problem was, he decided against finding a quick hook-up. Instead he went outside to wait.

He strolled back and forth in front of the club as vampires and fae went in and out of the building. Humans had always volunteered to donate their blood for the sexual aspect and thrill of it, but Ramiro had never taken the time to figure out why the fae did it. Was it purely sexual on their part? Ramiro couldn't imagine a fae needing the thrill.

"Okay, what's so important?" Audric asked, stepping out of the bar.

"I was wondering if you'd remembered any more about your wolf, and what you went through after being turned by LaMont?" Ramiro asked.

"Why do you ask?" Audric's eyes narrowed in suspicion. "No good can come of it."

"I think I may have found a way for Gunnar to hang on to that part of himself. So tell me why you don't think it's a good idea?" It seemed Audric agreed with Ian. Perhaps it had been wrong of him to talk to Gunnar about the possibilities.

"Because not being able to shift is equal to you starving for blood. It's a hunger that won't go away. To wish that on someone is to hate them, in my opinion." Audric's voice had gone down several octaves. It was more than obvious the man was pissed off at the very idea. "I had to bury that part of myself or risk insanity. Gunnar was a born Alpha. For him, the risk is even greater."

What had he done? "Thank you for your honesty." Ramiro needed to find Gunnar and drive all thoughts of holding on to his wolf from his head. "Excuse me, I have to go."

Before Ramiro could make a move, Audric's hand was wrapped around his forearm. "I know you're only trying to help him, but both of you need to accept what he's become."

"You're right. I understand that now." Ramiro took off, hoping it wasn't too late.

Chapter Two

Gunnar stared at the walls of his bedroom. Living in the palace with Spiro and Neo had proved to be important, but he missed the open space of the vineyard. He thought of the rest of the wolves and cats who'd been relocated to The Realm for their safety.

The sooner they put an end to Morwyn and the Galway Alpha, Juniper Cavanaugh, the faster he could get his people home. Gunnar fisted his hands. He could no longer claim the weres as his people. It had been the hardest thing to come to terms with. Belonging to and leading a pack had meant everything to him. His position as head of security for Neo had also been a question on his mind lately. Would the weres still respect and follow him?

Regardless of his future position, he still owed it to the weres to fight the upcoming war as if he were still their Alpha. Jumping up from the large bed he'd been given, Gunnar parted the heavy canopy drapes. There was research to be done if they were to have any hope of defeating Morwyn. His personal issues could wait.

He was on his way down to the palace vault when he spotted Ramiro. Gunnar did his best to duck around a corner before the vampire saw him. After their earlier kiss, the last thing he wanted was to tempt his body again so soon. He had no doubt it was the changes in his genetic makeup that wanted Ramiro and nothing more.

"We need to talk," Ramiro said, still hidden from view.

"I'm on my way to the vault. There are things more important than whether or not I can retain my wolf." Gunnar refused to cling to a dream he knew was unattainable. He'd had numerous discussions with Audric over the possibility that his wolf could survive the change. When Ramiro had mentioned the book, it had given Gunnar a spark of hope, but the kiss had quickly put things into perspective. He was a vampire.

Ramiro turned the corner and stared at Gunnar. "I'll go with you."

Gunnar took a step back before he realised what he was doing. He stopped and squared his shoulders. Had his Alpha been driven so deeply inside himself that a vampire intimidated him? No. Gunnar knew exactly why he'd retreated. How long would the battle rage between his body and his mind?

"Whatever," Gunnar finally said, continuing down the hall. He wove his way through the maze-like corridors with Ramiro right on his heels. Reaching the library, Gunnar nodded at the two guards and waited for them to open the massive doors.

Once the doors were shut behind him, he walked over to the statue of Zeus and pressed the small button on the underside of its beard. The floor opened to a spiral staircase that would take them to the vault.

As they descended the steps, Gunnar heard a noise from below. He stopped and glanced up at Ramiro. "There's someone already down here."

Ramiro nodded. "Probably Neo. He wants to get back to the vineyard as much as you do."

Mention of his home caused an ache in Gunnar's chest. He needed to speak to Neo about his job, but the upcoming war was more important. Continuing down the steps, he walked into the dimly lit vault. He'd been told the massive room was kept at a constant sixteen degrees celsius, eliciting a momentary body-shiver from Gunnar.

Neo glanced up from the book on the table in front of him. The expression on his face was grave. "Morwyn's drawing the underworld powers of the Titans."

"What?" Ramiro stopped beside Gunnar. "That's not possible."

Neo pointed to the book. "It is if he has this."

Gunnar exchanged glances with Ramiro before continuing to the table. He peered over Neo's shoulder at an ancient illustration. "Cronus's sickle? But I thought that was destroyed in the war against the Titans and Olympians."

"Not destroyed. Lost." Neo carefully turned the brittle pages of the book to another picture. This one depicted a scene from the Titanomachy, the great war of the Gods, Zeus charging Cronus and the sickle falling from Cronus's hand towards Earth below. "I think Juniper Cavanaugh somehow found it, whether he was already communicating with Morwyn or what, I don't know." Neo tapped the picture. "This has to be what rescued Morwyn from the bowels of Tartarus."

Gunnar started to ask how Neo had figured it out, but Neo stopped him.

"This is the only thing in existence other than my father's lightning bolts that have the power to unlock the door to Tartarus." Neo rose out of his chair. "There's something else."

Gunnar glanced at Ramiro before following Neo. "Are you telling us we have to get the sickle back if we want to banish Morwyn?"

"That's one way," Neo said absently. He continued to walk through the rows and rows of ancient texts until he reached the art area. "I can't find anything that confirms my suspicions, but there's a picture in here that's given me an idea."

Neo turned on a small lamp before opening one of the large, flat drawers used to house the original paintings. He turned and shifted his gaze between Gunnar and Ramiro. "You are two of the few who have ever been allowed in this area. What you see is for your eyes only. Am I understood?"

"Yes, sir," Gunnar answered immediately. He'd sworn allegiance to Neo long ago and, although he may lose his position once the war was over, his loyalties would always stand true.

After Ramiro had also agreed, Neo stepped back. "This is a depiction of the battle between Uranus and Cronus."

Gunnar wasn't sure what he was supposed to see. It was Ramiro who commented. "Just before his balls were lopped off, I gather."

Neo chuckled. "Yes." Neo moved over several rows before opening another drawer. "Now this one is of Morwyn's war with Nialo and the dragons. Notice anything?"

Gunnar reached out to touch the ancient canvas but quickly pulled his hand back. "The sword. It's the same."

"Yes. And according to history, the sword was never far from Morwyn's side. It's the same weapon he used to separate himself from Nialo." Neo pointed towards the canvas. "I believe Morwyn's looking for that sword. I think it's the reason he's assembling an army."

There was something in the way Neo said it that prompted a shiver to race up Gunnar's spine. A warm hand on his lower back told Gunnar that Ramiro sensed his unease. "Do you know where the sword is?"

"Hanging in a heavily-warded case over the fireplace in King Kildare's bedroom," Ramiro supplied.

Gunnar span around and stared into Ramiro's dark eyes, a spark of jealousy rising within him. Gods, he could easily get lost in those dark chocolate depths. He managed to find his voice, despite his body's reaction to the nearness of the vampire. "Why does he have it?"

"I don't know," Ramiro said, his focus on Gunnar's lips.

Dammit! Gunnar's cock hardened before he could turn away.

"Would you ask him?" Neo asked.

Ramiro glanced over Gunnar's shoulder at Neo. "Would you like me to set up a meeting?"

"Tomorrow evening, seven o' clock. I'll make sure Spiro's there as well." Neo shut the drawers before turning off the lamp. "We're running out of time. With each day, Juniper's army grows in size and strength."

* * * *

Just before dawn, Ramiro knocked on Ian's bedchamber door from his adjoining room. He was taking a risk by seeking audience with Ian at this time of the morning. Not only did Ian have a tendency to become crabby when he was forced to leave his playmates for a day of sleep, but he more than likely had a donor in his room for an early morning snack before bed.

When the door opened almost immediately, it was a surprise. "Come in," Ian beckoned.

Ramiro followed the totally nude King into his extravagant quarters. The sight of his firm ass didn't hold the appeal it once had for Ramiro, but it was still quite a work of art. He glanced towards the large fireplace, making sure it was, in fact, the same sword seen in the portraits.

Ian sat on the couch in front of the fireplace. He lifted his splayed legs and rested his heels on the sofa cushions, proudly exposing his hole to Ramiro's eyes. "What can I do for you?" he asked, his fingers circling the seldom-fucked pucker.

The erotic scene in front of him was almost more than Ramiro could ignore. For centuries Ian had played with Ramiro's affections, pulling him into bed before unceremoniously kicking him out again. It seemed Ian was in the mood to be taken, something he didn't allow anyone but Ramiro to do.

Before falling for Gunnar, Ramiro would've jumped at the chance to bury his cock in the King's ass again, but it no longer felt right. However, because of Ian's position, declining the apparent offer would mean the end of his career. Perhaps if he riled the King, Ian's attention would focus elsewhere. "Neo would like a meeting with you. He wants to discuss how you came about acquiring Morwyn's sword."

Ian jumped off the sofa and went to stand between Ramiro and the fireplace. "It's not Morwyn's sword! It belonged to Faelan. Morwyn stole it from him, and Faelan got it back when Morwyn was sentenced for his crimes."

Ramiro rubbed the back of his neck with his palm, trying to smooth the hairs that had begun to prickle. The vehement way Ian defended Faelan was unsettling. As far as Ramiro knew, Faelan had deserted Ian and the rest of the fae and vampires at around the same time Morwyn was exiled to Tartarus. "If Faelan feels so strongly for the sword, why do you have it?"

"It was a gift," Ian said defensively. "Not that I need to explain myself to you." Ian sniffed indignantly. "Tell Neo to forget the sword. It has nothing to do with this mess."

Ramiro's eyes narrowed. Was he being given an order? He'd sworn allegiance to Ian long ago, but how could he try and convince Neo of something he didn't believe himself? Better to think about it, he told himself. He bowed in respect for his king. "What shall I tell Neo about the meeting he's requested?"

"If you assure him about the sword, there will be no need for a meeting. Am I right?"

"Very well. I'll do my best." Ramiro turned and left the room before Ian's ardour returned. *Fuck!* He shut the door between rooms, unsure of what to do. *Faelan.* What part did the Creator's sword play in the upcoming war, or did it?

* * * *

Gunnar was in bed, asleep, when a touch to his chest woke him. His fangs slid from their sheaths as he lunged towards the threat.

"Control yourself!" Ramiro yelled as Gunnar knocked him to the floor, landing on top of him.

Blinking, Gunnar stared down at Ramiro. He released the hold he had on Ramiro's neck. "What're you doing sneaking up on me?"

"I needed to talk to you," Ramiro whispered.

The confused expression on Ramiro's face said it all. Gunnar swallowed around the lump in his throat. "What happened?" He slid off Ramiro to sit on the floor next to him.

"I'm worried."

Although Gunnar hadn't known Ramiro for long, he'd never seen the vampire so unsettled. "What about?"

Ramiro sat up and rested his forearms on his bent knees. "I'm being put in the middle of two leaders. One I've sworn allegiance to, and another I have the utmost respect for."

"Neo and Ian?" Gunnar knew Ramiro was supposed to set up a meeting between the two.

"Ian won't discuss the sword. He said it was a gift from Faelan and had nothing to do with Morwyn."

"But you don't believe him?" Gunnar ducked his head, trying to make eye contact with Ramiro. He wanted to reach out and offer comfort, but knew it would only lead to trouble.

"I don't know what to believe. Faelen's like this God of mystery. He hasn't even been seen or heard from since vampires came into existence. So it begs the question, is Ian telling the truth or is he lying to me because he knows I can't verify his answer?"

Out of nowhere, Ramiro growled and reached for the bed. He pulled a blanket to the floor before throwing it over Gunnar's lap.

Gunnar settled the blanket around his waist. His state of undress had been the least of his worries since Ramiro woke him. Although he refused to apologise, it was nice to know his nudity affected Ramiro even at a time of obvious distress. "Well, you'll have to tell Neo Ian refuses to meet with him."

"That's why I feel stuck in the middle. Ian didn't out-and-out refuse. He just told me to assure Neo the sword had nothing to do with Morwyn. I've sworn my allegiance to Ian, but if I do what he ordered me to do and it turns out he's lying, Neo will have my head."

"Why didn't you just ask Ian point-blank if he was planning to meet with Neo?" Gunnar asked.

"Because I had to get the hell out of his room before he made me fuck him, alright?" Ramiro barked.

Gunnar leant forwards, nose to nose with Ramiro. "He makes you fuck him?"

"I... He..."Ramiro sputtered. He took a deep breath. "Several times a year he wants me to fuck him. It was never an issue before..."

"Before?" Gunnar prompted.

"Before I met you." Ramiro stood. "I'll figure it out. Go on back to bed. Hell, I've got another four hours before the sun sets, and I have to face Neo."

The thought of Ramiro returning to Ian's palace didn't sit well with Gunnar. "You might as well sleep here — just stay on your side of the bed," he grumbled.

Ramiro actually chuckled, although it sounded strained. "Your generosity is overwhelming, but I brought my cape."

"Stay," Gunnar growled, holding the blanket around him as he stood.

Ramiro stepped forwards and pulled the blanket out of Gunnar's grasp. He stared into Gunnar's eyes as he reached down to run his hand over Gunnar's half-hard cock. "If I stay, there's no way in Hades I'll stick to my side of the bed."

"Would you rather be in Ian's?" Gunnar asked, jealousy coursing through his veins.

Ramiro's eyes narrowed to mere slits. "Don't push me. You've got me riding the edge of control right now. One more word and I'll bend you over the mattress and shove my dick up your ass."

The image of Ramiro fucking him flashed through Gunnar's mind. Conflicted, he turned his back towards Ramiro. "I guess you'd better go, then, because I'm no one's pussy-boy."

Ramiro bumped his chest against Gunnar's back hard enough to throw Gunnar off balance. Landing on the mattress, Gunnar quickly rolled over. His protest at the treatment was silenced by Ramiro's tongue thrusting into his mouth. Oh, Gods, the taste of Ramiro's kiss conjured images Gunnar was too proud to acknowledge. He opened further, accepting with pleasure the kiss that threatened to turn him from an Alpha to a beta. The thought shocked him. Gunnar pushed against Ramiro's shoulders, breaking the kiss. "You may not see me as an Alpha, but I do."

Ramiro grabbed the hair on the back of Gunnar's head, holding him in place. "Labels have no place in my bed," he growled. He released Gunnar before turning to stalk from the room.

Gunnar stared at the canopy overhead as he licked the last of Ramiro's flavour from his lips. He didn't expect Ramiro to understand. Vampires didn't think the same way weres did. But Gunnar had been labelled an Alpha at the young age of sixteen when he'd fought and killed his own father before walking away from the pack who'd never given him a damn thing except contempt.

"I earned that label, damn it!" he shouted to the empty room.

* * * *

Instead of going back to Ian's palace, Ramiro ended up in the vault once again, doing research. Hours into his labours he heard footsteps on the stairs. "Who's there?"

"Michael," a soft voice replied. "The guard told me you were down here."

Michael stepped into the room. His sleep-tousled blond curls and big, blue eyes made him look more like an angel than anyone Ramiro had ever seen. "Is it evening already?"

"Not quite." Michael rubbed his hands over his face as he sat across from Ramiro. "I like a few hours to myself before Neo's up for the night. What're you doing down here at this time of day?"

Despite Michael's young age, Ramiro had grown to respect the man's sensitivity and wisdom. "I'm trying to find information about Faelan," he admitted.

Michael's eyebrows shot up under the mop of blond hair. "Faelan? The only time I've even heard anyone talk about him was when I was still a boy. I'd asked Spiro where vampires came from and he told me the King of the Fae was afraid of the dark so he created vampires to watch over him while he slept."

Ramiro nodded. He'd heard a similar story, with a few differences. "I heard he was afraid of someone trying to kill him while he slept, but I guess you wouldn't tell a boy that."

Michael chuckled. "Especially not Spiro. He's always tried to protect me." Michael rested his cheek on his palm and yawned. "So what're you trying to find out about Faelan?"

"Where he is. His history." Ramiro shrugged. "I find it strange that he's barely mentioned." Ramiro did a broad sweep with his hands at the rows of books. "There are volumes of information about Blessed Creatures, Gods and demi-Gods in here, but I haven't managed to find a single book that pertains to Faelan. Why do you think that is?"

"Magic? Maybe Faelan doesn't want anyone to know his history. His powers must be extraordinary. I wouldn't think omitting his name from a few books would be hard with that kind of magic on his side."

"Possibly." Ramiro stared at the open book in front of him. "Do you think Spiro knows more about him?"

"He's half fae, so maybe," Michael supplied. He dropped his hands to the table and leant forwards. "Why is finding out about Faelan so important to you?"

"Because I don't think this war will be won on the battlefield. If we try to go hand-to-hand with those monsters Morwyn has created, not only will Blessed Creatures die, but the human population could easily be decimated. Especially if the Gods step in to the fight."

Ramiro didn't tell Michael he needed to know whether or not Ian was being honest with him. His doubts about the King he'd sworn allegiance to were his to prove or disprove.

"Neo said Zeus offered to go to battle with Morwyn, but the other Gods forbade it, knowing the toll such a battle would take on Earth."

Ramiro chuckled. "I don't see Zeus as the kind of God to take orders easily."

"That's exactly what I said to Neo. He told me that even though his father was a supreme asshole, he did seem to have a soft spot for Earth." Michael sighed. "It's the only thing either of us could come up with."

It had been Zeus' idea to house The Realm on Earth. Ramiro wondered if it was Earth itself, or its inhabitants Zeus was fond of. He yawned, his need for sleep apparent.

Michael chuckled and gestured to the back of the room. "There's a small bed I had brought down for Neo for his long days spent in here. Why don't you try to get a few hours in before the meeting?"

"There won't be a meeting. At least not with Ian," Ramiro admitted.

Michael bit his bottom lip. "Ooh, ouch. In that case, maybe I'd better go back up to bed, and make sure Neo's in a good mood before you tell him."

"I'd appreciate that," Ramiro said with a grin. "I'll try to catch a few hours of sleep."

After Michael had left the vault, Ramiro found his way to the double bed at the back of the room. With everything on his mind, he doubted sleep would come. There were too many unanswered questions, and his gut told him the truth lay at Ian's feet.

Finally, Ramiro felt the pull of sleep settle his overactive body and mind.

Chapter Three

Fresh from the shower, Gunnar answered the door without bothering with a towel. "Hey." He stepped back and allowed his visitor entrance.

Grinning, Audric came into the room. "You'd better dress before we're joined by two overly-jealous werewolves."

Nudity was commonplace in the were culture. Gunnar had seen Haig and Kern naked on numerous occasions, but he assumed it was different if their mate was in the room. He grabbed a pair of jeans out of the dresser and pulled them on. Rarely, if ever, did he wear underwear. It was a habit born from the need to shift at a moment's notice. "What brings you by?" he asked, pulling a T-shirt over his head.

"Just wondering if Ramiro talked to you last night." Audric kept his gaze on the landscape outside the window.

"Why would you ask that?" Had Ramiro gone to Audric after he'd left Gunnar's room?

Typical Audric—the vampire refused to look Gunnar in the eyes as he spoke. Gunnar knew Haig and Kern were trying to help the once-abused vampire gain confidence, but Gunnar could tell they had a long way to go.

"Ramiro told me outside The Frenzy about his desire to help you hold on to your wolf. You should probably know, I argued against it."

"Turn around and look at me." Gunnar couldn't stand the defeated posture of such a strong Blessed Creature.

Audric eventually did as asked. "I'm sorry. I know I shouldn't have stuck my nose into your business, but I've only just started to remember what I went through, and I don't want that for you."

Gunnar decided to sit down. Perhaps a less defensive posture would help put Audric at ease. Rubbing his hands together, Gunnar decided to be completely honest. "I'm having more trouble relinquishing my hold on my Alpha status than my wolf. Does that make sense?"

"No, and do you know why?" Audric asked, looking Gunnar in the eyes for the first time since he'd entered the room.

"Because my wolf has been with me longer than my status?" Gunnar offered.

Audric snorted. "No. Because being Alpha has nothing to do with your wolf." He shook his head. "Weres are so fucking conceited. Being an Alpha isn't exclusive to your wolf. It's who you are. It's about being the best in your particular group. I consider Ramiro an Alpha. If you'd put your heart into what you've become instead of what you were, no one would be able to take the title away from you. But you have to *want* it, and you have to *accept* who you are in order to get it."

Gunnar had never heard a vampire refer to himself as 'Alpha'. Was Audric right? Was he so conceited he'd discounted every other species of Blessed Creature?

Audric walked over and placed his palm over Gunnar's heart. "This is where a true Alpha lives." He moved to tap Gunnar's temple. "Not here. Because even in were form, your heart is always your own. It may be what drives the animal inside of you to excel in battle, but pure strength can't win the war."

No one had ever put it so directly and eloquently before. Given his new situation, Audric's words spoke directly to Gunnar's soul. "Thank you."

"You're welcome." Audric smiled. "Now you'd better change your shirt before Haig and Kern detect my scent on you."

* * * *

Gunnar purposely sat across the table and several chairs down from Ramiro as he waited for the meeting to start. He had noticed upon entering the conference room how agitated Ramiro seemed, and wondered whether Ian's Chief of Security was still pissed off with him.

The door opened and Haig ushered Galena into the room. He spoke softly to his sister before guiding her to a chair beside Kern. Although Gunnar had not taken part in Galena's rescue, he'd heard Ramiro mention the deplorable living conditions the mate of Juniper Cavanaugh had lived in.

As soon as she was seated, Galena lifted her feet onto the chair and curled her arms around her legs, rolling her body into a ball. Gunnar made eye contact with Haig, asking silently if the meeting was too much for the traumatised were.

Haig leant over and whispered in Galena's ear once more. Several moments later, Galena put her feet on the floor.

Before Gunnar had a chance to examine the situation further, Neo and Michael stepped into the room, followed by Spiro. When Spiro turned to shut the door, Sema head-butted the wood until he was allowed entrance. Spiro shook his head at the large black jaguar and pointed towards the corner of the room behind his chair. Sema went dutifully to the indicated spot and lay down.

"May I speak to you?" Ramiro asked Neo.

"No need. Michael already told me Ian isn't coming." Neo's restraint was visible. "I'll speak to Ian after the meeting. I'd like you to be there."

"Yes, sir," Ramiro answered.

"Would you like me there as well?" Gunnar asked. As Neo's head of security, it was customary.

"That won't be necessary." Neo returned his attention to Ramiro. "Tell me exactly what King Kildare said when you asked him about the sword."

Ramiro shifted in his chair. "He said the sword had never belonged to Morwyn. That Morwyn stole it from Faelan, but he managed to get it back when Morwayn was exiled to Tartarus. Faelan, in turn, gave it to Ian. According to Ian, the sword has nothing to do with the war."

Gunnar was still reeling from Neo's dismissal. Had he already been replaced? His gaze slid to Haig. The were appeared cool and confident, as usual.

"Gunnar," Neo prompted.

Gunnar looked away from Haig to find the entire table of Blessed Creatures staring at him. "Sorry. Did you ask me something?"

Neo's lips thinned with unspoken anger. He stood and indicated the door. "I need to talk to you out in the hall."

Fuck! Gunnar rose before following Neo out of the conference room. "I'm sorry," he said as soon as they were alone.

Neo's expression softened. "What's going on with you lately, besides the obvious?"

Gunnar stuck his hands in his pockets. Should he lay everything out for Neo or hold back? "Are you going to replace me?" he blurted out.

"I hadn't planned on it, but I'm suddenly questioning your commitment."

"Then why aren't you taking me to your meeting with King Kildare?" Did he think Ramiro was enough protection? *Surely not.* Ramiro may be working with Neo but he'd sworn allegiance to Kildare.

"I need answers from Ian, and if I show up with you, he'll immediately get defensive. Besides, I need you to gather your best men to surround the pack land in Galway. There's been a lot of traffic lately in and out, and I want to know why."

Neo's answers helped to soothe Gunnar's ego. "Will we be allowed to engage them should they step out of the ward?"

"No, not unless they attack first. I want Morwyn and Juniper to know they're being watched. You'll report everything back to me, Spiro or Ramiro."

"Why Ramiro?" Despite what Neo had told him only a few seconds earlier, it sounded to Gunnar as if Ramiro was Neo's new confidant.

Neo crossed his arms over his chest. "What's your problem with Ramiro? He's gone above and beyond anything I've ever asked of him. Damn, Gunnar, the man got you through the transition without even being asked. He's done more for you than probably anyone in your entire life. So why the disdain?"

Why indeed? "It seems as though he's trying to take my place, I guess."

With a heavy sigh, Neo uncrossed his arms before putting his hands on Gunnar's shoulders. "I can see why you think that, but honestly, I think he's just trying to pick up some of your slack. You have to admit you haven't been one hundred percent on your game lately. We all know the transition's been hard for you so we've given you time and space. Ramiro's trying to help you. Don't hate him for it. Thank him."

Gunnar's spine stiffened. He squared his shoulders and looked Neo in the eyes. "I don't need someone else to do my job. I'll have my men ready as soon as you give the word." He reached for the doorknob, but Neo stopped him.

"On a personal note, I have information that Rafi's been seen in Gort, a town just south of Galway. I can't talk about it in the meeting for obvious reasons, but I need you to find out what the hell he's doing there. I would never expect Juniper to work with a weretiger, but stranger things have happened."

Gunnar understood the personal nature of the request. The last time anyone had seen Neo's long-time lover, Rafi had physically attacked Michael. Before running off, the weretiger had sworn that one day Neo and Michael would be sorry for the way he'd been treated. "I'll poke around, and see what I can find."

"Thanks," Neo said before opening the door.

Gunnar noticed Ramiro watching him when he pulled out his chair to resume his seat. He met Ramiro's gaze and held it for several moments. A wealth of emotions coursed through him. When the corner of Ramiro's mouth turned up in a grin, Gunnar's cock hardened. Careful not to give his condition away, Gunnar broke eye contact and returned his attention to Neo.

Thirty minutes later, Haig ended his initial report on the years of abuse his sister had suffered during her marriage to Juniper. Numbed by all that he had heard, Gunnar noticed the way Galena failed to make eye contact with anyone at the table.

It was obvious by the silence in the room that Gunnar wasn't the only one affected by the horrific details. It was Spiro who spoke first, using a soft, non-threatening tone of voice. "Galena? Can you tell me if you've ever seen this?" he asked, before passing a copy of Cronus's sickle across the table.

Galena's gaze scanned the photo before shaking her head.

"Use your words, sweetheart," Haig encouraged with an arm around his sister.

"No," she eventually answered.

Gunnar noticed the brief, unspoken exchange between Spiro and Neo. Spiro drew back the picture and returned it to the folder. "Did Juniper ever mention Morwyn by name?"

Galena's blonde eyebrows drew together. "No." She glanced at Haig. "Although he sometimes talked about his Master. Right before Juniper put me in the cage, I came into the bedroom and Juniper was lying in bed talking to someone in a language I didn't know." Galena shook her head. "But there was no one else in the room. When I asked him who he was talking to, he told me the Master. The next day he had my cage built."

"The Master," Neo said aloud. "Is that the only name Juniper used?"

Galena nodded. "Yes."

The meeting ended shortly afterwards. Neo stopped Gunnar on the way out. "Michael's getting the supplies ready for you and your men. Spiro will accompany you long enough to place protective wards around your campsites."

"Do you want just the weres or should I call in some of the vamps from The Realm army?"

Neo scratched his jaw as he entered the hallway. "I'll leave that up to you." Neo pounded Gunnar on the back. "Despite what you seem to think, I still believe in your abilities to head this up for me."

"Thank you." It was the first positive reinforcement Gunnar had received since being kidnapped. "I won't let you down."

With a final nod, Neo turned the corner and disappeared.

"How long before you leave?" Ramiro asked, coming up behind Gunnar.

"As soon as I can muster the guards and brief them on the mission. Why?"

"I'm accompanying Spiro. Just wondered how long I had." Ramiro leant his hip against the wall. "I'd also like the chance to speak to you in private."

Gunnar knew Ramiro would need to leave soon for his meeting with Neo and Kildare. He motioned for Ramiro to follow him back into the conference room. Once Ramiro was in and the door was shut, Gunnar turned to face the gorgeous vampire. He had a few questions of his own. "Why'd you stay with me after Richard turned me?"

"Because you needed someone to help you through the transition, and I was the only one strong enough to control you."

"Really? That's the only reason?" Gunnar prodded. It wasn't just Neo who seemed to enjoy reminding Gunnar of everything Ramiro had done for him in those early days. Michael loved to wax poetic about how it was Ramiro's constant vigilance that had kept Gunnar from going insane during his transformation.

"What else are you willing to hear, Gunnar? So far every time I try to tell you something, you just push me away."

Gunnar realised Ramiro was right. "I don't mean to."

"Liar," Ramiro said, taking several steps towards him.

"You make me feel weak," Gunnar admitted.

Ramiro slowly shook his head. "No I don't. It's not weakness you feel. It's loss of control." Ramiro put his hand on Gunnar's hip, before sliding it around to rest on the small of his back. "Guess what?" he whispered against Gunnar's mouth.

Mesmerised by the dark eyes staring into his own, Gunnar could barely speak. "What?"

"Losing control isn't a bad thing when it's done with someone you trust." Ramiro kissed Gunnar's bottom lip, sucking the tingling flesh for several moments before releasing it. "I have no desire to control you. I just want to be with you."

Hard and aching, Gunnar ground his erection against Ramiro's. It felt much different from grinding against his hand or the mattress. He opened his mouth for Ramiro's kiss and tried to concentrate on the moment, pushing aside any lingering doubts. *I can do this.*

Ramiro must have sensed the moment Gunnar gave in, because suddenly the sexy vampire took things to the next level. Gunnar groaned into the deep kiss as Ramiro's strong hands began to squeeze his ass. "Want you," Ramiro growled, breaking the kiss to bite and suck Gunnar's lips.

Never had Gunnar experienced such passion in a lover. Of course his experiences were limited to quick fucks in the forest back in Norway. He'd not even had that since he'd killed his father. *Shit!* He quickly tried to push the memories away.

Once again, Ramiro seemed to sense his mood. He pulled back and stared into Gunnar's eyes. "Something wrong?"

Gunnar shook his head. He was so fucking mad at himself he didn't know what to say.

Ramiro kissed his way to Gunnar's ear. "Let me in," he whispered.

"There are dark places inside of me," Gunnar mumbled. How could he possibly admit to Ramiro that he'd murdered his own father?

"Darkness lives in all of us." Ramiro kissed Gunnar's neck while he lowered the zip on Gunnar's jeans. "Let me hold you in the dark."

Gunnar's eyes closed as he pressed his cheek against Ramiro's. Gods, he wanted to believe. The first touch of Ramiro's hand on his bare cock almost tipped Gunnar over the edge. *No!* He wouldn't let it end with him coming in Ramiro's palm. Spurred into action, he managed to open the fancy slide-hook on Ramiro's dress slacks before lowering the zipper. "I want to feel you wrapped around me when I come."

Ramiro's nostrils flared. He spat into the palm of his hand and reached behind his back. "Let me show you what trust really means."

Gunnar followed Ramiro's lead and slicked his aching cock with saliva. He was ashamed to admit he hadn't thought of lube. In wolf form, such niceties weren't a consideration when natural instincts called.

After several moments, Ramiro turned around. He braced his hands on the table before glancing over his shoulder. "Fuck me."

Gunnar swallowed around the lump in his throat as he stepped close enough to press the head of his cock against Ramiro's stretched hole. Should he say anything or just do it? It was yet another difference between fucking in fur versus flesh.

"Just do it. You won't hurt me," Ramiro encouraged, leaning farther over the table.

Gunnar held the base of his cock and pushed the crown of his erection through the outer ring of muscles. He gasped when Ramiro's body seemed to suck his cock deeper. Nothing in all his life had felt so good. Once his length was fully inside Ramiro, Gunnar placed one hand on top of Ramiro's shoulder while he rested the other on the vampire's hip. The urge to thrust soon became overwhelming. "Can I?"

"Please," Ramiro pleaded.

Gunnar pulled out until just the head remained inside before surging forwards. His stomach turned over at the sheer pleasure coursing through his body as he did it again. Soon he had a steady rhythm set. He gave up control to his instincts, aware that this part of fucking was the same no matter what form he was in. On each inward thrust, he began to grunt, and found he enjoyed the sound of his own voice taking pleasure in Ramiro's body.

"So good... So much better," Ramiro mumbled, reaching back to touch Gunnar's hip.

The phone in Ramiro's pants' pocket began to ring, interrupting Gunnar's rhythm. "Don't stop," Ramiro growled.

Gunnar picked up his pace once again, and tried to ignore the phone. It was Neo, no doubt. The thought of his time with Ramiro coming to an end before they both came was unthinkable. He released his hold on Ramiro's hip and wrapped his hand around the fat cock sliding across the tabletop.

Ramiro's body responded by squeezing Gunnar's cock on each thrust. "Can't hold it any longer," Gunnar warned, moments before the first strand of seed shot from his cock. Before he realised what he was doing, his fangs slid from their sheaths and sank into the soft flesh of Ramiro's neck. The blood that poured into his mouth was bitter, old tasting, pulling him back to his senses. He automatically licked the wound and waited for Ramiro to start yelling at him.

Ramiro's chest was flat on the table, and Gunnar realised his hand was not only sandwiched under his lover, but covered in cum.

"Sorry," Gunnar mumbled.

"Shhh," Ramiro said, trying to regain his breath.

It had been the first time Gunnar had actually bitten someone. He hoped biting a fellow vampire wasn't considered taboo. The thought froze Gunnar in place. *Fellow vampire.*

Acknowledgment of his realisation was on the tip of his tongue when Ramiro's phone began to ring. *Saved by the bell.* Gunnar pulled out of Ramiro's body and took a step back. "It's probably time for your meeting."

Ramiro turned around and pulled Gunnar into his arms. "Promise me you won't run away."

"I've got to get to Galway," Gunnar answered.

"You know what I mean." Ramiro pulled Gunnar in for a deep kiss. When his cell phone rang for a third time, Ramiro groaned and pulled away. "I'll be there in two minutes." He set the phone on the table and reached down for his pants. "Get your guards gathered while I take care of this issue with Ian."

"Have you decided whether or not Ian's telling the truth?" Gunnar asked, adjusting his clothes.

"No. I'm hoping Neo can draw out the truth." Ramiro opened the door. "Should I ask Ian about sending some of my guys with you?"

"I'll use vamps from The Realm detail. I'd rather not get too involved with Ian until we know where he stands." He started to pass, but Ramiro stepped in front of him.

"My guards are good men and loyal to *me*, first and foremost. If you need them let me know."

With one last peck on the lips, Ramiro was off, disappearing in front of Gunnar's eyes. He'd yet to learn that particular trick, but Ramiro had assured him it would come in time, once he'd fully embraced who he was. Gunnar wasn't at all sure it was worth it.

* * * *

Neo was waiting for Ramiro at Ian's palace gate. "It's about time."

"Sorry." Ramiro took a step forward and waited for the gate to open.

"So what's going on between you two?" Neo asked.

Ramiro didn't bother to play ignorant. "Gunnar's stubborn, but I think I'm wearing him down."

Neo glanced at Ramiro and grinned. "Shouldn't be too tough—I don't think he's had sex in centuries."

Ramiro pulled Neo to a stop before they reached the palace doors. Had he known, he'd have waited until they could spend more time together. "You're kidding me, right?"

Neo shook his head. "He's been at the vineyard for nearly two-hundred and sixty years and has a very strict rule about not sleeping with the weres who report to him. So unless he's sneaking off into the woods with one of the strays from town, he's celibate."

Not anymore. Ramiro knew that nugget of information would continue to nag at him until he spoke to Gunnar about it. He couldn't imagine a life without the touch of another male. Even the touch of a donor was enough to remind him he'd once been human. "I guess that could explain his growly disposition," he mumbled.

The doors opened and Neo and Ramiro were ushered inside. Ramiro greeted Ian's house steward, Allister. "Will you ask the King if he'll see us?" He could have gone to ask Ian on his own, but with an unannounced visitor in tow, Ramiro felt it was best to follow protocol.

"He hasn't come down yet this evening, but I shall see if he's available," Allister answered before going off in search of King Kildare.

While they waited, Neo walked around the reception room with his hands clasped behind his back. "Quite a place," he commented, staring at the gilded columns.

Ramiro smiled. Neo's vineyard home was vastly different from Ian's over-the-top decorating style. "Yeah, it's not for everyone, but I think it makes Ian happy."

"Well that's the most important thing, I guess." Neo span around when an alarm sounded.

"Ian," Ramiro yelled, before dashing up the winding staircase. In the hallway, just outside Ian's bedroom, Allister was bent over, a pile of vomit at his feet. "Where are the guards?"

Allister pointed towards the open door. "Dead."

Ramiro glanced over his shoulder at Neo before proceeding into the room. He stopped just inside the doorway, sickened by the scene in front of him. No wonder Allister was currently emptying the contents of his stomach.

The nude bodies of the two vampires assigned to guard the King's door were arranged on the bed. "This is all wrong," he mumbled. "Ian didn't fuck vampires." He knew he was the exception, but his past relationship with Ian wasn't in question. Besides, Ian had never fucked him.

Neo pointed to the two heads positioned on the mantel. "Yeah, I guess you could say that."

Ramiro glanced at the faces of two of his best guards, Rodrick and Warden. He couldn't help but feel he'd let his men down. His gaze zeroed in on the hooks that had once held the case containing the sword.

Ramiro ventured farther into the room. Other than the headless bodies on the bed, there were no other signs of a struggle. *What the hell are you up to, Ian?* Had the King been taken, or had Ian been the one responsible for the guards' death?

Neo must have been thinking the same thing. "How'd Ian act the last time you saw him?"

"Protective of the sword. I don't think he appreciated being asked about it." Once again, Ramiro chose not to tell Neo about Ian's desire to be fucked.

"He seemed adamant the sword wasn't Morwyn's though. What do you know about Faelan?"

Neo chuckled. "What does anyone know about Faelan?" He shook his head. "He's like the Phantom of The Realm. I've heard about him since I was a child, but only his name."

"What about Zeus? Could he tell us anything?"

"No. Now whether he really doesn't know anything about Faelan or just refuses to tell me I don't know, but I did ask."

It didn't make sense to Ramiro. If Faelan had the ability to remove himself from books and paintings, did he also fade memories of himself from the minds of Blessed Creatures? Ramiro turned from the fireplace and headed towards the hallway. He addressed the guards who had gathered. "King Kildare's missing."

"How?" one of the guards asked. "The ward should've stopped anyone trying to get past it without authorisation."

"Exactly," Ramiro mumbled. Did he dare voice his concern that Ian had killed the two vampires and disappeared with the sword? No, better to wait until he knew more. "I'll handle the King's disappearance. Until we find him, there's no need to guard the palace as we have been." Ramiro turned to address Neo, "My men are at your disposal if you need them."

"Thank you, I just might," Neo answered.

After giving orders for the removal of the two bodies, Ramiro followed Neo back to The Realm palace.

"Any ideas?" Neo asked on the way.

"My gut tells me it had to either be someone more powerful than Ian's ward or Ian himself."

"My thoughts exactly. So, that begs the question—who has the ability to get through Ian's ward?" Neo led Ramiro towards the library.

"Faelan or Morwyn, take your pick." The possible motive chilled Ramiro to the bone.

"Why not just take the sword? What would they need Ian for?" Neo pushed the button that revealed the hidden staircase down to the vault.

"You mean you don't know?" Ramiro was confused. He'd thought Neo knew everything about the Blessed Creatures.

"Know what?"

"Ian was the first. Without him, we would be the soulless creatures you see in movies. It's the reason I've dedicated my life to ensuring his safety." Ramiro knew Neo had never fully accepted his vampire side. "None of us asked to become what we are. If my service to Ian can help protect the souls of my brethren, I'll do everything in my power to guarantee his welfare."

Neo bit his bottom lip. It was obvious to Ramiro that Neo was unaware of Ian's importance to the vampire creatures other than being their king. "Then I guess we need to find him."

"Yes. It's possible he'll be used as a bargaining chip at some point. What better way to control a legion of vampires who value their souls?" The outcome, should something happen to Ian, was unthinkable.

"Are you coming down?" Neo asked from the top of the vault's staircase.

"No. I've got to meet up with Spiro. I tend to lose all sense of time when I'm in the vault," Ramiro explained.

Neo stared at Ramiro for several moments. "Will Gunnar be safe from the sunlight in one of the regular tents? I'm ashamed to admit I forget he's not were anymore."

"I've got a tent that's designed especially for vampires. I'll make sure he uses it."

"Good." Neo took several steps down. "I'll see you back here tomorrow evening."

Ramiro was surprised. "Are you sure you don't want me to accompany Spiro back?"

"He'll be fine once he leaves Galway. I'll let you know if I find anything out about Ian. For now, just…enjoy the time you have with Gunnar." It was easy enough to read Neo's mind. If something did happen to Ian, Ramiro wouldn't be the only one to lose his soul. "I could say the same thing to you. Why don't you ask Michael to join you?"

"Oh, I plan to," Neo chuckled.

Ramiro turned away from the vault's entrance. He felt like he was standing on the edge of disaster, but what could he possibly do about it other than enjoy the time he had?

Chapter Four

With the night drawing to a close, Gunnar stood beside Haig. "Keep an eye out for Rafi," he told his friend. There was only one road into the pack lands and it divided Gunnar's newly set-up camp from Haig, Kern and Audric's.

Haig nodded. "I heard." He glanced over his shoulder at Kern and Audric who were busy setting up the protective vampire-grade tent. "How much danger do you think we're in? The pack has to know we're here."

"Spiro's trying to finish up the wards around all our campsites. That'll protect us as long as we stay within the perimeter. As of right now, our jobs are to observe and report back to Neo, nothing more." Gunnar knew it was harder for Haig to remain calm while being so close to the were who had tortured his sister for centuries, but they still didn't know what they were up against. "If we're given the go-ahead to engage, believe me, we won't leave you out of the fight."

"I appreciate that."

Spiro appeared with Ramiro at his side. In full protective-mode, Ramiro made Gunnar's mouth water. Gods, he longed to run his hands over the vampire's muscled chest. Gunnar's cock hardened when Ramiro made eye contact. "Finished?" Gunnar asked Spiro.

"Yes, and just in time." He gestured at the horizon. "Sun'll be up soon."

"We need to get you back to your campsite," Ramiro told Gunnar.

Gunnar was slowly getting used to the change in his sleeping schedule. It didn't take long for him to figure out his strength diminished drastically at dawn. He knew Ramiro could go a day or so without sleep, but Ramiro had been a vampire a hell of a lot longer than he had. Gunnar slapped Haig on the shoulder. "Keep your eyes open and log everything you see. I'll check in with you this evening."

Gunnar started towards his campsite, eyes open for any sign of Juniper or his pack of monsters.

"Wait up," Ramiro called, jogging after him.

Gunnar glanced over his shoulder to see Spiro had disappeared. "Don't you have to accompany Spiro?"

"No. I'm here for the day," Ramiro said, falling in stride next to Gunnar.

"The day?" Gunnar's heart began to beat faster at the implication. Would they repeat their earlier actions?

Ramiro brushed his hand against Gunnar's thigh. "Is that okay?"

Gunnar's throat went dry. "More than."

Ramiro grabbed Gunnar's hand and led him inside the tent. He zipped the flaps against the first rays of sunlight, plunging the space into darkness.

"Guess this fancy tent of yours works," Gunnar said. He'd been directing his men on where to set up camp when Ramiro had arrived with the special light-blocking tent. Although he could see, his vision was tinted red. In wolf-form, Gunnar had seen through the darkness in black and white. The red was one more reminder of what he'd become. "Is there a lamp or something in here?"

"You don't need it," Ramiro reminded him, unbuttoning his shirt.

"No, I don't, but I think I'd prefer it." Gunnar watched as Ramiro moved to the corner of the tent and turned on a small battery-operated lantern. "Does that help?"

Gunnar nodded before pulling off his T-shirt. The bed was nothing more than a thick sleeping bag laid out with a blanket on top, but to him it was full of promise. Was he hoping for more than Ramiro was willing to give? *Probably*. But it didn't stop him from secretly wanting it.

Ramiro wasted no time in undressing. He dug a small tube of lube out of his jacket pocket and slipped it under the sleeping bag.

Gunnar could tell Ramiro was trying to be subtle. Knowing Ramiro's motives were to put Gunnar at ease made him trust the hot vampire even more than he already did. Their brief encounter earlier had left him hungry for more. But this time he was anxious to hold Ramiro afterwards. Something he hadn't desired for many years.

"Stop worrying," Ramiro said, pulling Gunnar into his arms. He brushed his lips across Gunnar's temple, ending the gesture with a soft kiss. "Feel me," he whispered in Gunnar's ear.

Gunnar closed his eyes when Ramiro slowly lowered his zipper.

"Lay down and I'll take off your boots," Ramiro instructed.

"I can do it," Gunnar returned.

"Of course you can. You've been doing for yourself for centuries, but now it's my turn to do for you." Ramiro knelt and began to untie Gunnar's military-style boots. "It's been a long time since I had someone to take care of."

Ramiro's voice was so soft, so gentle, Gunnar almost missed the pain in it. He wanted to argue that he didn't need taking care of, but something in that deep cadence stopped him. Who had Ramiro taken care of?

Ramiro stared up at Gunnar. "Lie down. Please," he added.

With his jeans pushed down to mid-thigh, Gunnar fell back onto the sleeping bag. He wanted to ask Ramiro about his past, but decided it wasn't the time.

Soon, Gunnar was naked and accepting a deep kiss. The brush of Ramiro's cock as he fitted himself between Gunnar's legs made him groan. Needing more, Gunnar wrapped his legs around Ramiro's waist. Gods, the press of Ramiro's cock as he ground himself against Gunnar was beyond anything he'd experienced in his short-lived sexual past. "Skin feels so much better than fur," Gunnar said, breaking the kiss.

Ramiro's hips stilled. "You say that like you've never done this before."

Although he hated to admit his lack of experience to someone as sexually active as Ramiro, Gunnar knew it was important to be honest. "Before yesterday, I'd never fucked in human form, and never face to face. Back home, there were a couple of like-minded weres, but it was forbidden. What we did, we did quickly and deep in the forest."

Instead of being disgusted, like Gunnar had assumed, Ramiro smiled. "Man, are you in for a treat."

After another quick kiss, Ramiro began licking his way down Gunnar's neck and chest. He stopped at each nipple to tease and bite before moving on. The attention made Gunnar squirm. It was too much and not enough. He nudged Ramiro's shoulders, hoping to feel that lapping tongue on his cock. "Please," he begged.

Gunnar was on the verge of giving up control, something he'd never done. As Ramiro moved further down his body, Gunnar began to worry. Would he always be at Ramiro's mercy? As Ramiro's tongue swirled around the head of his cock, Gunnar had his answer. Fuck, he could handle being on the receiving end of Ramiro's mouth for a few centuries.

Gunnar buried one hand in Ramiro's thick, black hair while he grabbed the base of his cock with the other. He needed to feel the vampire's throat. Once again, begging was in the forefront of his mind, but Ramiro quickly took the hint and swallowed Gunnar's cock.

"Ahhhh, fuck!" Gunnar yelled, thrusting deeper.

Ramiro released Gunnar's cock and chuckled. "If you plan to fuck me, I'd better back off."

It only took a moment's hesitation before Gunnar shook his head. "I want to know what it feels like to...you know?"

Ramiro smiled. "Yes, I know." He reached over to the hidden tube of lube. "It'll be easier for you on your hands and knees," he explained.

"No," Gunnar said with a shake of his head. "I want to feel like a man, not a wolf."

Ramiro took a deep breath. "Okay." He leant back on his heels and bent Gunnar's legs at the knees, placing his feet flat on the ground. "I'll go slow. Just tell me if you become uncomfortable."

Although Gunnar understood that Ramiro was trying to be gentle with him, the comment made him bristle. "I'm not a fucking kid. I know what's involved."

Ramiro grinned and held up his hands. "Fine." He squirted some lube onto his fingers and ran them down the crease of Gunnar's ass.

The moment the pad of Ramiro's middle finger began circling Gunnar's hole, he knew he was in trouble. Despite what he'd agreed to, Ramiro would no doubt draw the torture out for as long as possible. Gunnar lifted his legs, trying to figure out how to give Ramiro better access to his hole. Maybe Ramiro had been right and he should turn over.

"Hook your arms under your knees and lift them to your chest," Ramiro said, interrupting Gunnar's thoughts.

The moment Gunnar complied, he felt the first finger press against his hole. He bit the inside of his cheek to keep from crying out as Ramiro sank in to the second knuckle. It wasn't pain he felt at the intrusion, but the last of his reserve slipping away. He would do anything, be anything, if only he could know what it felt like to truly belong to someone.

Ramiro placed his hand low on Gunnar's stomach and added another finger to his ass. "Feel," he whispered.

Gunnar's hips jerked as Ramiro pressed against his prostate. Of course he'd found that pleasurable spot before, but it felt completely different when nudged by someone else. "Again," he growled.

Laughing, Ramiro prodded his prostate once more before withdrawing his fingers.

"Hey," Gunnar scolded.

One of Ramiro's black eyebrows rose. "Patience." He reached for the lube and slicked his cock, before positioning himself at Gunnar's hole. "I've thought of this. So many mornings I lay in bed and dreamt of this day."

Before entering Gunnar, Ramiro reached up and cupped his cheek. He opened his mouth, but no words were spoken. Closing it, Ramiro gave a slight shake of his head. "Ready?"

Unable to speak around the sudden knot of emotions in his throat, Gunnar nodded. He held on to his legs as Ramiro's cock pushed slowly inside. Although the pain was more than he'd expected, it wasn't the worst he'd ever experienced. Still, he had to wonder... "Does it get easier?" he finally asked.

Ramiro stopped. "It'll take your body a minute to adjust, but I promise it'll be worth it." He rubbed Gunnar's stomach. "Just relax and breathe."

Gunnar's eyes closed as his head fell back to the sleeping bag. He did as instructed and, within moments, the pain seemed to lessen. Sighing, Gunnar grinned. "You were right."

"Of course. Did you doubt me?" Ramiro asked, amusement in his voice.

Opening his eyes, Gunnar scowled. "Stop being smug and fuck me."

Laughing, Ramiro slowly slid in, an inch at a time, until Gunnar felt the vampire's balls press against him. "How's that?"

"Good," Gunnar answered honestly. "Damn good."

Ramiro stretched out, resting his chest against Gunnar's, and kissed him. "Put your legs around me," he whispered after breaking the deep tongue-probe.

Gunnar released his legs and groaned. "I'm too old to be a pretzel anyway."

"No you're not." Ramiro nipped Gunnar's bottom lip. He pulled out before pushing back inside. "But I prefer to feel you wrapped around me." Ramiro stared into Gunnar's eyes as he began thrusting in and out.

There was something unspoken happening between them, and Gunnar wondered whether he'd ever be able to walk away unscathed. Each time Ramiro sank deep into Gunnar's body it felt almost like a brand to Gunnar. Whether Ramiro knew it or not, it seemed vampires were capable of love because in that moment, Gunnar knew he was in love.

Only once before had he thought himself in love, but he now knew the truth. What he had felt for Brandr had been a crush, nothing more. He'd never lain with the older were, had never been asked. Why would a strong beta like Brandr look twice at a pup like Gunnar when he could have Gunnar's father?

Gunnar gasped at the rush of pain and emotion that threatened to overwhelm him. He'd long ago buried the memories of his life before leaving Norway.

Ramiro slowed his rhythm. "What's wrong?"

"Nothing. Just the past trying to break in to the present." He knew he would eventually have to tell Ramiro about the darkness that lived within him, but not yet. If their relationship continued to develop, he would lower his walls. He pulled Ramiro's head down for a kiss. He aggressively probed the interior of Ramiro's mouth with his tongue, hoping to drive away the demons that still haunted him.

Ramiro's thrusts increased in speed and intensity the longer they kissed. Perhaps Ramiro had his own demons to rid himself of?

Gunnar wrapped his legs higher around Ramiro's back, giving himself room to reach his cock. As the erotic tongue duel continued, he began stroking his dick. He was close. He just needed that little bit... Gunnar pinched the sensitive spot just under the head of his cock and erupted. His body jerking with the force of his climax, Gunnar broke the kiss and howled Ramiro's name.

"Fuck! So good," Ramiro yelled, loud enough for the entire region to hear. His body bucked as he filled Gunnar with heat.

Gunnar's eyes popped open at the warmth invading his persistently cold body. For the first time since he'd been kidnapped, he felt something other than the constant chill in his bones. "Heat," he gasped, still trying to catch his breath.

Ramiro chuckled. "Yes." He collapsed on top of Gunnar and kissed his neck. "There are only two things that can give vampires that kind of comfort, fucking and feeding."

"Why didn't you tell me?" Gunnar asked.

When Ramiro remained silent, Gunnar rolled until they lay side by side. "Answer me."

Moving to rest his head on Gunnar's shoulder, Ramiro licked his lips. "I wanted you to want me without incentives. Can you understand that?"

Gunnar nodded. "I needed to be ready," he surmised.

"Yes," Ramiro confirmed.

"But what about feeding? I've tasted your blood and it's obvious vampires aren't meant to feed from each other, so why not at least tell me about feeding from others?"

"Honestly? Same reason. I've seen vampires come to hate themselves for feeding on the living because they were forced into it too early. I wanted you to love it as much as I do, but for the right reason, not just to feel warm."

"Why *do* you love it?" Gunnar asked. He'd watched vampires feed and never understood the draw. It seemed...cheap, like trading sexual favours for money or, in the case of a vampire, blood.

Ramiro's fingers wandered across Gunnar's chest to his right nipple. "According to Ian, vampires were created to be aggressive, ruthless soldiers to protect Zeus and The Realm. After Ian was created, he was sent out to capture and change others, and they in turn brought even more vampires into existence. Unfortunately, once the threat from Morwyn was no longer an issue, there was little use for vampires and they were released into the world. So although vampires were suddenly free, they still had killer instincts."

Ramiro brushed his thumb back and forth over Gunnar's nipple. "LaMont was also one of the first created by Ian, and we both know what kind of vampire he was."

"Sadistic," Gunnar mumbled, thinking of the torture Neo had gone through at LaMont's hands.

"Yes. Some of the vampires were willing to adapt to life among humans. They were quick to discover humans would welcome a bite if they were given pleasure in exchange. For the vampires it was a way to get what they had to have while still fulfilling their need to dominate their prey." Ramiro leant in and kissed Gunnar's collarbone.

Gunnar tilted his head to the side. "Do you have to fuck them though?" he had to ask.

"No, but until you, I didn't have anyone else in particular I wanted to fuck." Ramiro released the skin between his teeth and gazed into Gunnar's eyes. "I like to fuck."

Ramiro's hand travelled from Gunnar's stomach down to his inner thigh. Gunnar held his breath each time Ramiro's thumb grazed his sac. "I'm not here for a one-time thing. I can get that at The Frenzy."

"Don't remind me," Gunnar growled. He grabbed Ramiro by the back of the neck and pulled him forwards until their lips barely touched. "I won't share."

"Outside of what is required to feed, neither will I," Ramiro said before sealing his lips to Gunnar's.

Gunnar accepted Ramiro's tongue. Feeding was necessary, he knew that, but did that mean Ramiro would continue to fuck his food? It would be a problem between them unless they could come to an arrangement. Gunnar considered himself a fair person, but could he really compromise on something so important to him?

* * * *

Ramiro woke before Gunnar. Although the sun was sinking lower over the horizon, it wouldn't be healthy for Gunnar to emerge from the tent's shelter until it was completely set. He pulled on his wrinkled pants and shirt before venturing outside into the cool rain.

The thought of Gunnar sitting out all night in the cold, wet Irish climate troubled Ramiro. Hands on his hips, he looked around the area. He spotted Haig in the distance and decided to have a quick word with him.

Ramiro closed his eyes and focussed on the signature of Haig's unique energy. He'd learnt to harness his gifts from Ian, and doubted there was another vampire, besides the King himself, who knew exactly what vampires were truly capable of. He felt the wind blow through him as he vanished from Gunnar's campsite to join Haig.

"Damn it! Warn a guy next time," Haig growled.

"Sorry." Ramiro tried to cover his smile by turning his head and glancing back towards Gunnar's camp. He didn't need to ask where Kern was. The erotic sounds coming from the tent made him uncomfortably hard, especially knowing there was a naked vampire only a few hundred yards away.

He turned his attention back to Haig. "Have you seen anything?"

Haig snorted. "Only a small army of those fucking freaks staring at me from the trees."

Ramiro had gone into the Galway camp with Neo to rescue Galena, so he understood why Haig referred to the hybridised weres as freaks. "Did they try to engage you in any way?"

"No. They just stared at us. I gotta tell you, knowing what those bastards did to my sister, it took everything I had not to charge them. Promise me if it ever comes to battle, you'll let me lead the fight."

Ramiro respected Haig's need for vengeance, but he also knew it wouldn't be a wise decision. "How about this? If and when we get the go-ahead to engage, I'll make sure you're with us. However, we both know Neo won't sit back and let us fight without him."

Haig dipped his head. "Juniper?"

"Neo and I already talked about that. We have a few questions for Juniper, but after we're done with him, he's all yours."

"Thanks."

The noise in the tent ended. The silence reminded Ramiro of why he'd come over in the first place. "Do me a favour and keep an eye on Gunnar's camp. I don't like him being alone at night, but I've got to find Ian. I'll be with him during the daylight hours, but he'll be on his own the rest of the time."

"No he won't," Kern said, coming out of the tent. "Gunnar's always been there for me and Haig. We won't let anything happen to him."

Ramiro squeezed Kern's shoulder. "Don't let him know you're watching him."

Haig and Kern both laughed. "We've worked for Gunnar a long time," Kern said. "No need to warn us about his temper."

Ramiro acknowledged the relationship Gunnar had with his guards with a nod of his head. "I'll leave you to it. See you in the morning." He didn't wait for an answer. Within a split second he was inside the tent, standing in front of a half-dressed Gunnar.

"Dammit!" Gunnar shouted.

Ramiro laughed. "That's exactly what Haig said when I popped in to his camp."

"What were you doing over there?" Gunnar asked, pulling on his T-shirt.

"Just checking in. He said Juniper's freaks stared at them all day. Make sure you keep a close eye on the trees."

Gunnar grabbed Ramiro around his waist and pulled him in. "Don't worry about me. I've got to go into town anyway, to try and catch up with Rafi."

"Let me do that," Ramiro offered.

"Neo asked me to do it," Gunnar argued.

"I know, and I'll talk to him about it first, but it's safer for me. The thought of you going all the way into town without the protection of a ward is too much for Neo to ask of you, especially here." Ramiro knew he was taking a chance. His relationship with Gunnar was too new to know how the newly-turned vampire would feel about his protective streak.

Gunnar stared off into space for several moments before answering. "I'll do whatever Neo wants me to do. To be honest, I'm not sure Rafi would give me any information anyway. When he left, he didn't think much of anyone at the vineyard."

Ramiro leant in for a kiss. He would have loved to spend the evening sitting around a fire with Gunnar, but there were too many things to be done. Once the danger was behind them, he hoped they would have a long time to enjoy their nights together.

"I need you to promise me something," Gunnar said, breaking the kiss.

"If I can," Ramiro answered.

"When you get back to The Realm to feed, no fucking."

"Didn't plan on it. I'll be back here in less than twelve hours anyway. I think I can control myself that long." It bothered Ramiro that Gunnar felt the need to ask. It would definitely be something they would have to discuss further.

Chapter Five

Soaked to the bone from the constant light rain, Gunnar continued to watch the treeline. Although he couldn't see anyone, he could definitely smell them. The odour was a combination of raw sewage and rotting meat. "Where are you, you bastards?" he whispered.

Gunnar continued to wait, bored out of his mind. He'd already spent the first couple of hours thinking about Ramiro. If it hadn't been for the eyes he knew were watching him, he would have taken out his aching cock to relieve himself.

Movement in the trees brought Gunnar to his feet. All at once, the trees seemed to step closer. "Fuck!" It wasn't the trees, it was Juniper's freaks. Shoulder to shoulder, a line of freaks began to march towards him.

Suddenly, Audric appeared inside the protective ward of Gunnar's camp. "Thought you might need some backup."

"Do you see the size of those bastards? I don't think backup is going to help me much if they've figured out a way to get past Spiro's magic."

"There must be at least a hundred of them," Audric mumbled. "Should I wake Kern and Haig?"

Gunnar glanced towards Audric's camp to see the two weres scrambling out of their tent, half-dressed. "No need. I think they smelt them coming."

"Shit. Be right back."

In an instant, Audric was gone. Gunnar was beginning to see the upside to being a vampire. He really needed to learn that particular talent. Pulling out his phone, he called Ramiro.

"Hey," Ramiro answered.

"Something's happening. I've got about a hundred freaks coming my way."

"Shit. I'll call Neo and be right there."

Gunnar shoved the phone back into his pocket just as Audric appeared with Kern and Haig. "Ramiro's on the way."

"Good. He's the only one of us who knows what Juniper looks like," Haig said, stepping to the edge of the ward.

"They don't look like they're out for our blood," Audric commented.

"No, they don't. As a matter of fact, they look more like zombies than living creatures. Look at their eyes. There seems to be nothing behind them." Gunnar felt a hand on his lower back and turned to find Ramiro standing just behind him.

Ramiro ran his hand down Gunnar's ass. "Neo's on his way, despite Michael's very vocal protests."

Gunnar felt his cock begin to harden at the brief touch. No. It wasn't the time. He tried to focus on the threat marching their way. "What's wrong with them?"

"They have no soul," Neo answered.

Gunnar turned to face his boss. "How is that possible?"

"Evidently it's the price they've paid for their increased size and strength." Neo moved to stand beside Haig. "Under no circumstances are you to step outside this ward, you understand?"

Haig's hands fisted at his sides but he eventually nodded his acceptance of the order.

Gunnar leant against Ramiro and whispered in his ear. "Do you see Juniper?"

"No." Ramiro flicked Gunnar's earlobe with his tongue before pulling back.

When the freaks were a mere ten yards from the ward, they stopped, as if by silent command. One of the biggest men Gunnar had ever seen took a step forward. "Why are you here?"

"To watch you," Neo said, suddenly appearing beside Gunnar. "Where's Morwyn?" he asked the freak.

"You are being asked to leave. I suggest you heed the warning."

"Or what?" Neo asked. "What is it Morwyn wants?"

The spokesman took a step back into line. As one, the army did an about-face and began to march back to the trees.

"You tell Juniper Cavanaugh to get his sissy ass down here and talk to us!" Haig shouted.

"So we've been warned." Neo rested his fists on his hips. "Gods! I wish we could get another look inside their operation."

"Maybe we can," Ramiro said. "When Gunnar called, I had just started my conversation with Rafi."

Gunnar watched as Neo's spine seemed to stiffen. "Did you find out what he's doing here?" Neo asked.

"According to him, he wants to help us," Ramiro answered.

"Do you believe him?" Gunnar asked.

"I don't know. I mean, I don't know him. He sounded earnest, but he said he wants to speak with Neo."

Gunnar's protective instincts kicked in. It suddenly didn't matter that his boss and friend was the son of a God. No good could come of a meeting between Neo and his ex-lover. "You can't. Not only is it too dangerous, but Michael would never understand," he said, his gaze on the army melting into the darkness of the trees.

All at once, the empty camp where Audric, Kern and Haig had been moments before exploded. Thrown to the ground by the force of the blast, Gunnar shielded his eyes from the bright fireball that climbed towards the clouds.

One moment, Ramiro was on the ground beside him, and the next he had thrown himself on top of Gunnar. Although Gunnar enjoyed the feeling of the vampire against him, he didn't appreciate the gesture. Pushing against Ramiro's chest, he tried to get the muscled security chief off him. "I don't need your protection," he growled.

Ramiro rolled off Gunnar. "I didn't...," he sputtered, getting to his feet. He held out his hand and helped Gunnar up. "I acted without thinking. I apologise."

Neo walked over. "You two okay?"

"Yeah," Gunnar answered. "What the hell was that?"

"Morwyn letting me know he means business. Ramiro, find Rafi and bring him to The Realm. I'll deal with Michael if he has a problem with it." He looked over his shoulder at the obliterated campsite before addressing Gunnar. "We need to get the guards back to The Realm. Now. We'll have to figure out another way to keep an eye on Juniper. Perhaps it's time to bring my father into this."

* * * *

Ramiro stared at the handsome weretiger across the conference table. It had taken a good deal of convincing for Rafi to allow Gunnar and Ramiro in the room when he spoke to Neo. The one concession he wouldn't relent to was having Michael in the room.

"What do you know about what's going on in Juniper's pack?" Neo asked.

"Not much. One of Juniper's men talked to me at the bar in Gort a couple of days ago. Said they were looking for other Blessed Creatures to join them. I played it cool, didn't want to seem too eager. I asked the guy what was in it for me, and he told me they'd been promised free reign on Earth if they were victorious in battle."

Ramiro leant forward, bracing his forearms on the table. "Did he tell you anything about the sword?"

"No. He didn't mention a sword." Rafi reached across the table towards Neo. "I'll join them and find out everything I can if you ask me to."

Neo pulled his hand back out of Rafi's reach. "I'm sorry, but I can't ask you to do something when I'm not willing to give you what you want in return."

"All I want is to do whatever's necessary to keep you safe. I know you don't want me, but I still..." Rafi shook his head. "I'll help. I've got nothing else to believe in."

Neo glanced up from his clasped hands. "Gunnar, would you and Ramiro give me a moment alone with Rafi?"

"Alone with him? No, I don't think it would be wise," Gunnar returned.

Neo narrowed his eyes. "I can assure you, I know how to take care of myself." His head tilted to the side. "Or have you forgotten who I am?"

Gunnar's head jerked back as if he'd been punched. "No." Gunnar stood without another word and strode from the room.

Standing, Ramiro stared down at Neo. He wanted to give Neo a piece of his mind for the words that had obviously hurt the man he loved, but he knew he couldn't. However... "I realise Gunnar is your employee, but I believe he was speaking out of what he believed was friendship."

"Not that I need to explain myself to you, but I didn't mean what I said the way he took it," Neo tried to explain.

"Yeah, well, tell him that." Ramiro walked out into the hall just in time to see Gunnar round the corner. "Fuck." The last several days had gone a long way in restoring Gunnar's self-confidence. Ramiro feared Neo's hasty words had set Gunnar back everything he'd gained.

He took off at a jog, catching up with Gunnar before he reached the palace doors. "Gunnar."

Gunner slowed his pace. "I need to get out of here for a while."

"Okay. Mind if I join you?"

Gunnar shrugged. "I won't be good company."

"I'm used to it," Ramiro said, hoping to lighten Gunnar's mood.

With a smirk on his face, Gunnar waited for the guard to open the door. Once outside, he headed in the direction of the park.

Ramiro reached for Gunnar's hand and was pleasantly surprised when Gunnar offered no resistance. As they walked, Ramiro could feel the tension draining from Gunnar's body. Although he hadn't planned to talk to Gunnar about his feelings quite so early in their relationship, something told him it was the right time.

When Gunnar started down the main path, Ramiro gave his hand a tug. "I've got something I want to show you." Ramiro led Gunnar over the barricade and onto the soft grass.

"You're going to get us in trouble," Gunnar mumbled.

Ramiro stopped and pulled Gunnar into his arms. He leant in and rimmed Gunnar's lips with the tip of his tongue. "I am trouble." He ended the statement with a deep, probing kiss, ready to shout to the universe his intention of keeping the vampire in his arms. *Gods, when did I become such a fucking sap?*

Breaking the kiss, Ramiro smiled. "Come on, it's through the trees."

Once they had reached the small copse of trees, Gunnar pulled Ramiro to a stop. "Give me a second." He tilted his head back and let the moonlight filtering through the leaves bathe his face. Again, the longing of his old life came back in full force. He missed roaming the forest in his wolf skin, the feel of the ground under his paws.

"This wasn't where I was taking you, but you look rather content. Let's go sit on that rock," Ramiro offered.

Gunnar would rather have wallowed in the dirt and leaves at his feet, but decided if Ramiro could compromise, so could he. At least the boulder was flat and smooth. Gunnar wasted no time in spreading out on the rock with his arms out to the sides. "I love that smell," he mumbled.

"Dirt?" Ramiro questioned.

"Dirt…leaves…all of it." He rolled his head to the side to stare at Ramiro. "Once all this is over, I don't think I care to ever see another city. I dream of buying a piece of wooded land and building a house." He grinned at the mortified expression on Ramiro's handsome face. "What, that doesn't appeal to you?"

Ramiro seemed to school his expression. "What about the vineyard?"

Gunnar shrugged. "I'm not sure that's an option any longer."

"You should talk to Neo. He said he didn't mean what you think he did." Ramiro moved to curl up against Gunnar's side.

"He's my boss. I think he made his position quite clear," Gunnar stated, remembering the reprimand he'd received earlier.

"I've had time to think about it, and I believe he meant he was the son of Zeus. He was telling you he had no reason to be afraid of Rafi, because he was stronger."

"You really think so?" A large part of him wanted to believe Ramiro.

"I do." Ramiro kissed Gunnar's neck.

"He was right, you know. Sometimes I do forget who he really is. I guess I just get complacent in our relationship. I tend to think of him as a friend, not a demi-God."

"I know. I felt the same way about Ian. I hate that I don't know why he left or where he is." Ramiro rested his forehead against Gunnar's chest, curling himself around Gunnar's body.

Gunnar stroked Ramiro's back, hoping to give the vampire comfort. He decided to ask the question that had been on his mind since he learnt of Ian's sudden departure. "What if it turns out he's working with Morwyn?"

"I don't know. Ian's no saint. I've always known that, but I protected him anyway. I've seen him create and then kill vampires on a whim, but I had to believe there was more good in him then bad."

"Why would you risk your life for someone like that?" It didn't make sense to Gunnar. Sure Neo had faults, but Gunnar rarely questioned his friend's ethics.

"Because we're all tied to him. If keeping Ian alive means all vampires keep their souls, it's worth it. None of us asked for what we've become. Risking my life to ensure his safety is the least I can do for the rest of you."

"Do you really believe our souls are tied to him? What if he's lying?" Gunnar had heard a lot of stories about the Blessed Creatures over the years but that didn't make them all true.

"Why would he do that?"

"Can you think of a better way for him to gain our loyalty?" Still wrapped in Gunnar's arms, Ramiro went perfectly still. Gunnar knew it wasn't easy to think of a friend as a liar, especially about something as important as one's soul.

"I need to find him," Ramiro finally said.

"Do you have any idea where he may have gone?" Gunnar asked.

"No, but maybe with Spiro and Neo's permission, there's a way."

"How?"

"The Royal Donors are tied to Ian. The reason it's forbidden for any vampire to share a donor with the King is because of those ties. If I feed from one of them I'll be able to locate him."

"So why didn't you do that earlier when you first found the bodies of those guards?"

Ramiro began kissing Gunnar's neck and for a few delightful moments, Gunnar assumed he didn't plan to answer the question. When Ramiro's hand travelled down to lower Gunnar's zipper, Gunnar couldn't have cared less whether he received an answer or not.

With his cock free, Gunnar pulled Ramiro on top of him. "Need to feel you," he moaned, thrusting up against the hard bulge in Ramiro's suit pants.

Ramiro reached between them and within moments his bare cock rubbed against Gunnar's. "That what you needed?"

"Hell, yes." When the boulder under him started to scratch as his flesh, Gunnar stilled and allowed Ramiro to rub and grind against him. "You feel so good."

"Mmmm, so do you," Ramiro said right before he thrust his tongue in Gunnar's open mouth.

Because Ramiro hadn't pushed his pants out of the way, the fine wool material continually rubbed against the underside of Gunnar's sac. Gunnar grabbed Ramiro's butt and squeezed. His middle fingers delved into the crack of Ramiro's ass and brushed the sweet hole he was becoming addicted to.

When Gunnar pressed the tip of one finger against the hole, Ramiro's body bucked against him. Breaking the kiss, Ramiro actually whimpered as he shot his seed between them. It was the erotic aroma of his lover's cum mixed with the forest's natural scent that pushed Gunnar over the edge. "Fuck!" he ground out.

After several moments, Ramiro groaned and rolled off Gunnar. He pulled a handkerchief out of his pocket and wiped Gunnar clean before taking care of himself. "I need to talk to Neo before dawn. If I'm going to find Ian, I'll need to feed at dusk."

"Why do you need Neo's permission to feed?" Gunnar asked.

"Feeding from Ian's Royal Donors is punishable by death. If I do this, I'm going to need some kind of protection."

Gunnar's skin broke out in gooseflesh. He'd long ago made the decision to put his life on the line for what he believed, but to hear Ramiro say he'd do the same fuelled a protective instinct in Gunnar like he'd never known. "No. I can't let you do that."

"Yes you can." Ramiro leant down and placed a quick kiss on Gunnar's lips. "I'm damn good at my job, and Ian is my responsibility."

Gunnar couldn't argue the necessity of what Ramiro felt he had to do. His protest was completely personal. He simply wasn't ready to let Ramiro go yet. There were so many things he wanted to know and experience with Ramiro. "Can I go with you when you talk to Neo and Spiro?"

"Yes. You need to get a few things straight with Neo anyway."

"I consider Neo a friend worth fighting for so I've no doubt we'll work out our problems. It's you I want to be there for. Right now ensuring your safety means everything to me," Gunnar admitted.

Ramiro cupped the side of Gunnar's face. "And I feel the same way about you. I want to spend the rest of my days sleeping at your side."

Gunnar leant in to Ramiro's gentle touch. "I'd like that."

* * * *

Gunnar stood in the corner of the conference room with his arms crossed. It hadn't taken long for Neo and Spiro to agree to Ramiro's plan. Although they had promised his safety for the act itself, they could not promise a safe return if he decided to go after Ian after learning all he could from the Royal Donor's blood.

When the donor was brought in, Gunnar ground his teeth. The slim man draped in a red, sheer robe was breathtaking. He knew Ramiro had specifically requested the man because he was one of Ian's favourite food sources. Protests were on the tip of Gunnar's tongue, but he managed to hold his words at bay. Understanding Ramiro's reasoning behind the chosen donor didn't mean he had to like it.

A chuckle from beside him got his attention. Spiro was openly watching Gunnar and had obviously read Gunnar's emotions. "Relax," Spiro whispered. "It is but a single bite."

"Easy for you to say," Gunnar returned without thinking. Spiro had never had a special someone in his life. Only a select few knew Nialo, Morwyn's twin, was to be Spiro's mate.

With his left hand slowly stroking Sema's black fur, Spiro sobered immediately. "Yes, you're right, of course."

"Please excuse my hasty reply," Gunnar apologised.

Spiro shook his head. "It is I who should apologise. I spoke without knowledge."

Sema took the opportunity to nuzzle against Spiro's hip. It seemed even a black jaguar could sense Spiro's unhappiness.

Gunnar returned his attention to the ongoing activity in the room. Ramiro had explained the need to bring the Royal Donor to orgasm at the precise moment he inflicted the bite. It wasn't something Gunnar was unaware of, but hearing Ramiro describe step by step the process he would use to bring the donor's fulfilment was much easier than actually watching it take place.

Ramiro turned his head and made eye contact with Gunnar as he continued to jerk the donor's cock through the robe's opening. "Feel my hand," Ramiro mouthed silently.

Gunnar felt an unseen hand wrap around his own cock. As his cock hardened, Gunnar wondered how many tricks Ian had taught Ramiro over the years. More importantly, he seethed over where the lessons had no doubt taken place.

A deep, rumbling noise came from Ramiro's throat as the unseen hold on Gunnar's cock tightened. The sound and action drew Gunnar out of his head to focus squarely on the pleasure his beautiful vampire was providing.

"Aahhh." Gunnar let the moan slip from between his lips.

Suddenly aware of what was happening, Neo turned himself and Michael around to face the wall. He whispered something in Michael's ear and his mate nodded, draping an arm around Neo's waist.

Gunnar leant against the corner at his back and thrust his hips, pressing his cock against the unseen hands. He couldn't stop his body's reaction to Ramiro's touch. He quickly unzipped his jeans, afraid of coming in his clothes. He pulled the handkerchief, Ramiro had handed him earlier, out of his front pocket, understanding suddenly dawning on him. Ramiro had known exactly what he'd planned to do. He'd also known what Gunnar's reaction would be.

When his release came, it was the Royal Donor whose cries were heard echoing in the room. Gunnar caught the majority of his seed in the soft, white material and stared as Ramiro's sharp fangs slid with ease into the donor's artery.

What happened next surprised everyone in the room. Ramiro's body began to jerk as he fed. Sweat, something unseen on vampires, began to run from his pores.

"Enough!" Gunnar yelled, running forward. He pulled Ramiro away from the donor heedless that his lover's teeth would rip the donor's throat open if not extracted properly. Pulling Ramiro into his arms, Gunnar held his love who continued to suffer the mysterious effects of the donor's blood.

Neo rushed forward and quickly licked the Royal Donor's neck in an effort to save the man's life. Callous or not, Gunnar cared only for Ramiro's welfare. He lowered Ramiro to the floor and looked up at Spiro. "What's wrong with him?"

Spiro knelt beside them and put a hand to Ramiro's forehead. He closed his eyes and did whatever it was Gunnar had seen him to in the past. When Spiro opened his eyes, he transferred his hand from Ramiro's head to Gunnar's shoulder. "He's in no physical pain. Whatever he's going through is mental, but he seems to be coming down from it."

Gunnar continued to rock back and forth with Ramiro held against his chest. He glanced up long enough to see the Royal Donor alive but understandably weak. "I didn't mean to hurt him," he told Neo.

"I know." Neo put a hand on Michael's arm. "Get one of the guards to take the donor back to Ian's palace." He turned to the donor. "Thank you for your gift. Hopefully it will allow us to find your Master."

Gunnar's chest tightened at the term Master. As soon as the donor was out of the room, he vocalised his thoughts. "Galena said Juniper referred to whoever is behind this as Master. Do you know anyone else who requires their subordinates to call them that?"

Neo shook his head. He turned his focus to Ramiro, whose breathing had begun to return to normal. Squatting beside Gunnar, Neo tapped Ramiro's cheek. "Ramiro? Can you hear me?"

It took several moments, but eventually Ramiro's eyelids fluttered a few times before opening. He stared at Neo. "Did you know?"

"Know what?" Neo asked.

"Faelan's trapped inside Ian's body."

In an uncharacteristic move, Neo reared back, throwing himself off balance. Ass on the floor, Neo shook his head. "How's that possible? Faelen created Ian."

"No. Gaia created Ian, sealing Faelen forever into the body of a vampire."

Sema chose that moment to walk over and begin bathing Ramiro's face with his tongue. Ramiro sputtered and tried to push the jaguar away, but Sema wouldn't budge. "Back," Spiro commanded.

Although Sema stopped licking Ramiro and glanced back at Spiro, he still refused to do as he was told.

"What the hell his wrong with him?" Neo asked.

"I have no idea. I've never seen him like this before." Spiro moved to wrap his arms around Sema's neck in an attempt to physically move the jaguar away from Ramiro. Sema turned his head and nuzzled his face against Spiro's neck, but refused to remove himself from his position.

Before Gunnar could stop him, Ramiro lurched forward and buried his teeth in Sema's neck, just above Spiro's hold. Spiro released Sema and began trying to pull the vampire off the beloved pet.

"He's gone mad," Spiro claimed.

Ramiro released the jaguar and wiped the blood from his cheek. "I'm not mad, but you may be when I tell you what I know."

Sema gave Ramiro one last look before backing up to settle against Spiro's lap. Before returning his attention to Ramiro, Spiro thoroughly checked Sema's neck for injuries. "Why did you do that?"

"I had a feeling he was trying to tell me something," Ramiro admitted. "And I was right." Ramiro smoothed his hair away from his face. "Whatever magic holds Faelan inside Ian is also holding Nialo inside Sema."

Gunnar's jaw dropped. For hundreds of years he'd played with and talked to Neo's pet without realising Sema probably understood every word that had come out of Gunnar's mouth. He couldn't help but to think of his own wolf being trapped inside a body he could no longer shift from. The thought of Nialo being trapped broke Gunnar's heart.

Spiro appeared to be in shock at the news. Gunnar reached out and placed a hand on his friend's lean back. "Spiro?"

Without warning, Spiro jumped to his feet, upsetting Sema onto the floor. In the blink of an eye, Spiro was gone, leaving the rest of them to wonder where he'd gone. Sema let out a pained roar and ran from the room.

Neo stood. "I'm going to get some answers," he announced before disappearing.

After his mate and his surrogate father vanished, Michael broke into tears. "I don't understand what's going on. Nialo's a God. Who has that kind of power?"

Gunnar shuddered at the idea.

Chapter Six

Lying beside Gunnar, Ramiro couldn't get the images of Ian out of his head. The person he'd sworn to protect with his life was creating soulless freaks in Galway, right under Ramiro's nose. The chaos caused by Ian's actions would have severe repercussions if Zeus and the other Gods stepped into the fight. What would happen to vampires if Ian was found guilty and exiled to Tartarus.

He rolled to his side and watched Gunnar sleep. He'd waited too long to experience the kind of love he felt for Gunnar to give up without a fight. Gunnar's theory that Ian was lying about vampire souls being connected to his life was just that, a theory. Ramiro simply couldn't take the chance that Ian was telling the truth.

Throwing off the covers, Ramiro kissed Gunnar's temple before getting out of bed. He dressed quickly in a simple pair of jeans, something he rarely wore, but were more appropriate for what he had in mind.

He eased the door open and slipped into the hallway. Although Neo and Spiro had both returned just before dawn, they had refused to speak with anyone, choosing instead to lock themselves in the vault.

Ramiro headed towards the library, knowing he was taking a risk. He was surprised to find Sema asleep outside the library doors, flanked on either side by one of The Realm's guards. Ramiro wasn't sure if the guards were there to protect Sema or keep him from entering the library. "I need to speak with either Spiro or Neo."

"They asked not to be disturbed," one of the guards replied, looking straight ahead.

"I'm planning to locate and join King Kildare. Do you really believe they would want me to do that without at least talking to me first?"

The guards exchanged glanced. "One moment." The smaller of the two ducked inside the library, leaving Ramiro outside.

Ramiro took the opportunity to squat and make eye contact with Sema. "If you can hear me, Nialo, I'll find a way to release you," he promised.

Sema's head butted against his arm in reply.

Ramiro stood when the library door opened. "They'll see you now," the guard said.

Ramiro didn't waste time getting inside and down the vault steps. Spiro and Neo were sitting next to each other at the table. "Thank you for seeing me," he said upon entering the room.

"What choice did we have? Malcolm said you were on your way to find Ian." Neo sat back in his chair and crossed his arms over his chest.

"He's with Juniper. I think if I follow his signal, I can get by the ward," Ramiro stated.

"It's too dangerous," Spiro argued.

"Maybe, but it's better than waiting for him to make his next move."

Spiro swept his long white hair over his shoulder. "That won't be necessary. Zeus has finally agreed to handle the situation."

The statement left Ramiro with a sinking feeling. "Where does that leave the vampires?"

"Excuse me?" Spiro questioned. "Is your loyalty to Ian so deep you would follow him to his death?"

"Absolutely not. Ian fooled everyone, including me. I would hope the two of you know that."

"We do," Neo growled, sneering at his brother. "We don't believe Ian told you the truth about his link to vampire souls."

"How can you be sure? Look at the creatures he's created in Galway. You yourself determined they were without souls. Would you condemn an entire species to the same fate without being one hundred percent sure? My goal was to bring Ian back for trial before the Gods in the hope that his life would be spared."

Neo's eyebrows drew together. "After everything he's done you wish to spare him?"

"No. I wish to spare my brethren. What exactly has Ian done? He created a species of monsters, yes, but they haven't done any damage. He blew up a campsite that held no one. I don't know what Ian's after, but I don't believe vengeance for what he's done is worth risking the souls of many."

"Zeus believes it was Gaia who cast the spell on Sema," Spiro said.

"Why? Did he say?" Ramiro knew he was overstepping his position by asking such a personal and high-level question, but he needed to understand.

"No, but according to Zeus, Gaia is the only one with enough power to contain a God in such a way."

"Can he ask?"

Neo chuckled. "Even Zeus is not allowed to speak to Gaia directly. He can put the question out into the universe, but it's Gaia's choice whether or not to answer. Zeus suggested we find out from Ian."

"I can find him, so let me bring him here for questioning," Ramiro pleaded.

Neo shook his head. "Zeus already knows where he is."

Ramiro took a deep breath. Defeat wasn't something he accepted easily, but Neo and Spiro obviously didn't want his help. "You don't need me at all then. Is that what you're trying to tell me?"

Neo closed the book in front of him. "The situation has gone beyond what you're capable of helping us with. Quite frankly, Ian's more powerful than you are. If we were to send you after him, we'd be sending you to your death."

"And we're not prepared to do that," Spiro added.

"So I'm just supposed to sit back and hope you don't end up killing him? Because I don't think I can do that. I'd rather risk my own life then the souls of thousands." The tension in the room rose dramatically, but Ramiro stood his ground, shoulders squared.

Neo stood, his anger evident by not only his expression but his body language. Ramiro knew the demi-God wasn't used to being challenged. Before Neo spoke a word, Spiro stepped between them to address Neo.

"Perhaps Ramiro could be in the room when we question Ian." Spiro glanced over his shoulder at

Ramiro. "Would you leave us to apprehend Ian if such a promise was made?"

"We don't need his permission," Neo barked. "We're trying to save his life!"

"And I'm trying to preserve my soul!" Ramiro fired back. He returned his attention to Spiro. "I accept your offer with gratitude."

Spiro put a hand on Neo's chest. It was rare the brothers touched, so the significance of the gesture wasn't lost on Ramiro. "Ramiro may not have your power, but he has your heart. You both need to recognise what's at stake should we fail to procure Ian safely."

Neo stared into his brother's eyes, his body visibly more relaxed at Spiro's touch. "Yet another reason you're better at governing the Blessed Creatures. Where my instincts are to fight yours are to understand."

Spiro removed his hand. "I've had many years of practice. It'll come to you, my brother." He stepped out from between Ramiro and Neo. "Ramiro will back off in his pursuit to capture Ian, and you will get special concession for him to attend Ian's trial on Olympus. Are we agreed?"

"I agree to try. Zeus isn't someone who often makes deals with Blessed Creatures," Neo said. "Maybe it'll help if I tell him you're my choice to become the new Vampire King."

The announcement broadsided Ramiro. "No. I've learnt a lot in the past few months, primarily that Blessed Creatures are better off under a single ruler, or in your case, rulers. Dividing loyalties doesn't work."

Neo's held tilted to the side. "Most vampires would've jumped at the chance to become king. The fact that you put what's best for your brethren first and not your own ambitions only cements my decision."

Ramiro shook his head. "Although I'm extremely flattered, again, I must decline the position." His thoughts strayed to Gunnar. "Can you imagine Gunnar living in a palace, attending formal functions?"

Neo smiled. "So it's like that is it?"

"Yes. If he'll have me," Ramiro confessed. "His dream is to live in the forest. I intend to do whatever it takes to give him what he desires."

Neo slapped Ramiro on the shoulder. "Then you'll be living at the vineyard, because I don't plan on letting my head of security leave Le Uve del Regno any time soon."

"That's up to Gunnar. I know he hasn't felt secure in his position lately."

"I know. That's my fault, something I intend to remedy as soon as the current crisis is resolved." Neo lifted the book from the table. "If you'll excuse us, we're due for a meeting on Olympus."

Ramiro was left not knowing what to do. Should he follow Neo's advice and take a few hours off? He thought of the man upstairs nestled in a nice warm bed and grinned. Perhaps taking a break wouldn't be so bad after all.

* * * *

"Tell me again why you enjoy this?" Ramiro asked.

Gunnar chuckled. Night fishing wasn't nearly as fun as spreading out next to a pond in the sunshine, but it was something he needed to get used to. "I like to fish. You're the one who said we could do whatever I wanted."

"Yes, but I thought you'd chose something a little less…dirty." Ramiro brushed bits of grass off his suit pants.

Gunnar bumped his shoulder against Ramiro's. "As long as we can stay here on the vineyard, I don't care what we do." Gunnar took a deep breath. The grapes had started to ripen, and although Neo had hired labourers from town to tend the vines in his absence, they weren't doing a very good job. He wondered what Neo's reaction to his beloved Le Uve del Regno would be upon his return.

"Take me for a walk," Ramiro suggested.

"Okay. Where do you want to go?" Gunnar asked, reeling in his line.

"Show me your favourite spot."

Gunnar set his pole down before standing. "That's an easy one." He glanced down at Ramiro's expensive leather shoes. "You might get those dirty."

Ramiro rose and began to thoroughly brush off his clothes. "Guess I'll be forced to buy some hiking boots and overalls if I'm going to continue to spend time here," he mumbled.

Gunnar took Ramiro's hand and led him towards the trees. Growly or not, he liked the idea of Ramiro spending time at the vineyard.

The moment they stepped into the forest, Gunnar sighed. "Feels good to be home."

"Does it bother you?"

"What?"

"Being here and not being able to shift?"

Gunnar stopped in a small clearing and thought about the question. If it were anyone else, he would downplay his physical reaction to his old running ground, but Ramiro deserved so much more. "It's hard to explain. I think more than anything, I miss running with a pack. Even though I tried not to pal around with the men I work with, when we were in wolf form, I felt part of the group." He shrugged. "So, yeah, I guess I miss it, although my body doesn't ache to change like it did in the beginning, my heart longs for that sense of belonging."

Ramiro stepped in front of Gunnar and wrapped his arms around his waist. "You belong with me now. The big question is will I be enough for you?"

Once again, Gunnar gave it some serious thought before answering. "I need to tell you something before I can answer that." Gunnar stepped back and took Ramiro by the hand once more. "But first I want to take you to my spot."

Gunnar led Ramiro down a winding path. "Not much further," he said over his shoulder.

"Thank the Gods," Ramiro mumbled.

Deep in the timber was a small clearing with a rock-lined fire circle in the centre. "Here it is," he said, pulling Ramiro down to sit beside him on the smooth wooden bench he'd made nearly a hundred years earlier. "This is where I spend most of my time when I'm not working."

Ramiro looked up, but the majority of the night sky was hidden behind the tree canopy. "You know, in another hundred years or so, you'll be able to sit out here in the daylight hours for small stretches of time."

Gunnar had grudgingly given up hope of ever stepping outside during the day. "Really?"

"Yes." Ramiro turned sideways to straddle the bench. "Maybe sooner if you wear a strong sun block." He rested his chin on Gunnar's shoulder. "Is this where you'd like to build a house?"

"Hell, I'd give anything for that, but this is Neo's land and he won't allow it." Gunnar had even mentioned to Neo not long after he started work for him that someday he'd like to build a house in the woods. Neo hadn't agreed. He'd explained to Gunnar the importance of leaving the forest intact.

Ramiro brushed a kiss across Gunnar's cheek. "Maybe we can change his mind." He sucked Gunnar's earlobe into his mouth. "Neo wants something from me. Perhaps I'll use this piece of land as my bargaining chip."

Gunnar's spine stiffened as jealousy crept into his mind. "What does he want from you?"

"He wants me to be the new Vampire King. I told him no, and I don't plan to change my mind on that, but perhaps with the right incentive, I could be persuaded to retain my position as security chief."

It was a reminder of Neo's obvious respect for Ramiro. "Where will that leave me?" Gunnar asked.

"Right here where you belong." Ramiro turned Gunnar around until they faced each other. "With me," he whispered against Gunnar's lips.

"Neo won't need two heads of security on Le Uve del Regno."

"I won't be working for the vineyard. I'll probably be overseeing vampire affairs, but I can just as easily do that from here." Ramiro suddenly jerked back. "Unless, of course, you don't want me here."

Gunnar sighed. It seemed he wasn't the only one feeling insecure. He tried to think of a way to make Ramiro understand. Gods, he wished he was better at saying what he felt. "I want you here. I'm just not sure that I deserve you."

"Does this have something to do with the darkness that you claim lives inside of you?" Ramiro asked.

Gunnar knew the time had come. "Yes." Gunnar turned away, unable to look Ramiro in the eyes. "My father was the Alpha of my pack. Things happened, and I killed him."

When Gunnar said nothing more, Ramiro prompted him. "You can't just stop there. I know you wouldn't have killed someone for no reason. What did he do?"

"He had an affair with his Second-in-Command, Brandr." Gunnar took a deep breath. "Evidently Brandr wanted to more than a side fuck for my father because he cornered my mother while out on a hunt and killed her. When my father found out, he tore Brandr to shreds. I was young, but I thought I was in love with Brandr despite what he'd done, so I challenged my father and won." Gunnar shrugged. "I walked away from the pack that night and haven't been back since."

Ramiro's hand began to rub the small of Gunnar's back. "We've all done things we're ashamed of. It's hard to live for centuries and not have a few skeletons in your closet. Right or wrong, what you did was a long time ago. I think you've more than made up for it."

Gunnar couldn't help but feel relieved. "Are you always so damn optimistic?"

"I learned the hard way what guilt can do to a person. Believe me, you have to learn to let it go or it'll continue to fuck up your life."

Gunnar wondered what skeletons Ramiro had in his closet, but the mood had been heavy enough for one night. "We'd better get back to The Realm."

"We still have another hour or so before dawn," Ramiro said, pulling Gunnar's T-shirt over his head.

"Can you do that little transporting thing straight to bed when we're done?" Gunnar asked, lifting his hips so Ramiro could remove his jeans.

"I think you're ready to learn how to do it on your own." Ramiro knelt between Gunnar's legs and ran his tongue up the length of Gunnar's cock.

"Mmm, I'd rather learn my lesson tomorrow," Gunnar said with a groan.

Ramiro's mouth captured Gunnar's crown. Gunnar braced his hands by gripping the back side of the bench and thrust his hips, burying more of his length in Ramiro's mouth. The squeeze of Ramiro's throat as he swallowed more of Gunnar's erection was just what Gunnar needed. The only thing missing... "Do that mind thing with my hole." For someone who didn't think he'd ever let his guard down long enough to feel a cock breach his hole, Gunnar had quickly become addicted.

Ramiro released Gunnar's cock. "I'd rather touch you the old-fashioned way."

"Then get naked," Gunnar instructed.

While Ramiro removed his clothing piece by piece and laid it carefully on the bench, Gunnar slid to the ground. The small clearing had little grass due to the decreased amount of sunlight it received, which didn't bother Gunnar a bit. He enjoyed the soil and leaves as much as a patch of soft grass. He tossed several small sticks towards the fire-pit before spreading out on his back.

"You don't really expect me to get down there with you, do you?" Ramiro asked.

"You can stretch out on top of me when the time comes. Wouldn't want you to get dirty or anything." Gunnar grinned up at Ramiro and spread his legs. He was certain he looked like a wanton slut, but at the moment, that's exactly how he felt. Gone was the Alpha who'd always felt he had to posture. At least with Ramiro, Gunnar knew he didn't have to prove his position as a warrior.

Gunnar stretched his arms out to the sides, burying his fingers in the soft soil. The contact seemed to make his skin tingle. Was it just his imagination or could he truly feel the presence of his wolf? It had been too long since he'd felt that part of himself.

"What's wrong?" Ramiro asked, kneeling between Gunnar's spread thighs.

Gunnar shook his head. The talk he'd had with Ramiro and Audric came immediately to mind. If he admitted he still longed for his wolf and actually felt his presence, Ramiro would probably insist on taking him back to The Realm right away. He buried his hands further into the Earth. "Nothing. Just need you."

Ramiro stared at Gunnar for several moments before pulling a small tube of lube from his pants' pocket. "You really are happy here, aren't you?"

"Yes." Gunnar's fingertips began to ache, but he refused to remove them from the home they'd found in the dirt.

Ramiro's lubed fingers skated over Gunnar's hole several times before settling where Gunnar needed them most. "You're so damn sex..." Ramiro cut himself off midsentence and jumped to his feet. "Someone's here."

Gunnar was about to tell his lover to relax when he heard the rustling of the leaves. The smell hit him next. "Smell that?" he asked, sitting up. When he pulled his hands from the ground, he noticed the claws where his fingernails should be. "Shit!"

Ramiro glanced away from the forest. "What's? Oh, fuck!" he exclaimed upon seeing Gunnar's hands.

"Something like that," Gunnar agreed. He reached down and scooped up handfuls of dirt and began rubbing it on his chest, neck and face.

"What're you doing?" Ramiro asked.

Gunnar noticed Ramiro's fangs had slid from their sheaths at the incoming threat. "If it worked for my hands, maybe it'll work its magic on the rest of me. Right now we need all the help we can get."

"I should get you back to The Realm."

"Don't you dare. I don't need you to whisk me off to safety. We've waited too long for Juniper to make a move like this." When his chest began to tingle, Gunnar knew his wolf was fighting like hell to shift. Dropping to the ground, he began burrowing under the fallen leaves, rubbing his entire nude body against the soil.

Ramiro raced back to the bench and found his phone amongst the pile of clothes. "We've got company," he said into the phone before tossing it back to the bench.

Thoroughly covered from head to toe in dirt, Gunnar resumed his position next to Ramiro. "How many do you think there are?"

"Too many. We don't know how to kill them." Ramiro glanced at Gunnar. "If something happens, know that I love you."

"You picked a hell of a time to tell me that," Gunnar said as pain shot through his body. He doubled over before falling to his hands and knees. He could hear Ramiro's voice but the pain was too intense to make out the words. Fuck, what had he got himself into? Gunnar began to wonder whether he'd survive the transformation.

"Juniper!" Ramiro shouted.

Gunnar opened his eyes in time to see a group of monsters enter the clearing. He tried to get to his feet, but his body wouldn't cooperate. It was a cry of pain from Ramiro that allowed Gunnar's wolf to push to the forefront. All at once, hair sprouted through the pores on Gunnar's body as the crunch of shifting bone grew louder.

Staring down at his hands, Gunnar took a deep breath. He hadn't fully changed. Two-inch talons sprouted through the flesh of elongated, hairy human hands. An unexpected blow to his side knocked him over.

Instinct kicked in and Gunnar jumped to his feet, or what could pass as feet. They, too, seemed to have suffered through the partial shift. He swiped at the monster that had charged him and ripped easily through the freak's leathery flesh.

The monster charged once again as blood ran from the gaping wound on its chest. Gunnar hadn't noticed it at first, but he stood eye to eye with the thing. With the freak's size taken out of the equation, it was down to a battle of skill.

Although Gunnar received a bite to the forearm, he pushed through the pain to plunge his sharp claws through the hybrid's chest and into its beating heart. Before the freak fell to the ground, a searing pain ripped down Gunnar's back. He span around and lashed out at another of Juniper's hybrids.

All around him, the battle between Juniper's freaks and guards from The Realm raged on. Dodging blows and delivering lethal blows, Gunnar worked his way towards Ramiro. By some miracle, his wolf had come out to help protect the handsome vampire, and unless he hurried, it would all have been for nothing.

On the ground, Ramiro's muscles strained in his effort to hold a hybrid from ripping his throat open. Gunnar ended the lives of two more monsters before he reached the man he loved. One hard kick to a freak's head managed to get him off Ramiro. Gunnar charged towards the hybrid, ready to end his life as easily as he had the others.

"Stop!" Ramiro yelled. "It's Juniper," he informed Gunnar.

Gunnar barely heard Ramiro as he hoisted the freak that had dared to attack Ramiro off the ground.

"Gunnar, stop!" A deep voice ordered.

Seconds away from ending Juniper's life, Gunnar paused long enough to glance over his shoulder at Neo. Despite Gunnar's agitated state, an order from his boss had the ability to get through to him.

With Neo at his side, Spiro rushed forward. "Drop him," Spiro said.

Gunnar threw Juniper to the ground as hard as he could. Although it seemed he wouldn't be allowed to kill Juniper, the wolf inside him wanted to inflict more pain on the threat to its mate.

Juniper landed with a satisfying sound of breaking bones. Spiro shoved Gunnar out of the way and began a furious chant, moving his hands back and forth above Juniper's body. In the blink of an eye, Juniper was gone along, with Spiro.

"Where'd they go?" Gunnar asked, as clearly as his elongated muzzle would allow.

"To a holding cell," Neo explained.

"You're hurt," Ramiro said, turning Gunnar around to examine his back. "I need to get him out of here," he told Neo.

Neo glanced around the clearing, littered with bodies. "Sure, there's nothing left to do here but clean up the mess."

Once the immediate threat was handled, Gunnar's body began to change. Shame filled him at the reminder of what he must look like. He tried to walk away, but Ramiro stopped him.

"Are you okay?" Ramiro asked.

Gunnar shook his head. "Don't look at me." Although he couldn't tell for sure, Gunnar had a feeling he bore a striking resemblance to the dead hybrids.

"Close your eyes and hang on." Ramiro wrapped his arms around Gunnar.

When Gunnar opened his eyes, they were in his palace bedroom. "Stretch out on your stomach while I find Spiro."

Although his body felt like it was back to normal, his shame remained. He shook his head. "I'll be fine. There's still enough were in me to heal."

Ramiro reached for Gunnar's hand and pulled him towards the bed. "Don't do this. What happened out there was a fucking miracle. Don't let your pride turn it into something to be ashamed of."

Gunnar sat next to Ramiro. "I looked like them, didn't I?"

"Sort of," Ramiro answered. "But if it hadn't been for your wolf coming to my rescue, I'd be dead. So as far as I'm concerned, you never looked more beautiful to me."

Even though Gunnar knew Ramiro was lying through his teeth, the statement warmed him. He realised he hadn't had the chance to return Ramiro's earlier proclamation. "By the way, I love you, too, you handsome little liar."

Chapter Seven

Ramiro rubbed the sleep from his eyes before entering the conference room. Neo had summoned him out of a deep sleep for an emergency meeting. When he'd asked about waking Gunnar, Neo had told him to let Gunnar sleep.

Stepping into the room, Ramiro faced Neo alone. "It's just us?"

"Yes," Neo yawned. It was obvious he hadn't been to bed yet. "The trial is set for this afternoon at three. Zeus wants to get Ian out of the way as soon as possible. He's called upon Gaia, but so far nothing from her."

"So you found him?" Ramiro was surprised at how quickly Neo had apprehended Ian. It didn't gel with what he knew of his the King.

Neo tucked his hair behind his ears. "Zeus, actually. That's the reason I called you here. I got permission for you to sit in the gallery at the trial. I need you to listen for any inconsistencies in Ian's story. I can't get past the idea there's something deeper going on here."

Ramiro nodded. "I have the same feeling. If it was really Ian who constructed the ward around Juniper's pack land, his magic has to be stronger than he's ever let on. If that's the case, why would he let himself be so easily captured?"

"Exactly," Neo agreed. "The magic has to be coming from Faelan, but why is it surfacing now after all these centuries?"

"What does Spiro think?"

Neo shook his head. "We haven't talked much. He's obsessed with the idea that his destined mate is trapped inside Sema. At the moment, he can't seem concentrate on anything else for more than a few minutes at a time. Clasping his hands, Neo leant forward on his forearms. "What exactly did you see or feel when you bit Sema?"

Ramiro thought back to the incident. He'd tried to push the ordeal from his mind and had no desire to repeat it. "Images, mostly. A crying woman with strange green eyes. She was holding a handsome man with long black hair at one moment, and Sema the next." Suddenly a forgotten detail came back to him. Ramiro met Neo's gaze. "It was the same woman that I saw when I bit the donor. Only she wasn't sad at all, she was furious. The eyes were the same colour but held hatred instead of love."

"Gaia," Neo whispered. "I remember my mother telling me all the shades of green on Earth were the same colour as the flecks in Gaia's eyes."

"So you think it *was* Gaia who imprisoned Nialo inside Sema?" Why would a God with so much love for the man in her arms do such a thing? It didn't make sense to Ramiro. Neo appeared deep in thought. "Is that all?" Ramiro asked, ready to get back to bed.

"How's Gunnar?"

"Ashamed, I think. He doesn't like what he shifted into out there." He'd heard Gunnar crying in the shower earlier, but he hadn't intruded. Gunnar was one of the proudest Alphas Ramiro had ever met, and he knew he wouldn't be welcomed at such a rare emotional moment.

"Do you think he'll be okay?" Neo asked.

"Of course," Ramiro defended Gunnar. "As a matter of fact, I believe he's an even bigger asset to you now."

"I wasn't asking as a boss. He means more to me than that," Neo returned, anger and a touch of hurt in his voice.

Ramiro recognised his mistake too late. "Forgive me." He cleared his throat. "It's been a long time since you've talked to him. He notices, you know? I think it's the reason he doesn't believe you trust him anymore."

"I've been busy."

"I realise that. Perhaps after the trial you could find the time to sit down with him and work things out. I bet he would enjoy taking you fishing."

Neo made a face. "I hate to fish. Never understood the point of it."

"Me neither. I was hoping to get out of future outings."

"Not going to happen. It's the price you'll have to pay for being with him."

Ramiro grinned. "Then I'll gladly put on my overalls and work boots to accompany him."

Neo yawned. "I think I'll try to get a few hours of sleep before the trial. Do you think Gunnar will be upset that he'll not be allowed in Olympus?"

"I don't think so. We talked about it earlier, and he understands why I need to look Ian in the eyes.

Besides, three o'clock is too early in the day for him to be out."

"It wasn't easy to get you a seat in the gallery, so do us both a favour and be as discreet as possible." Neo stood and stretched his arms over his head. "I'll talk to Gunnar, I promise."

"Thank you." Ramiro followed Neo out of the room. "Will Michael be accompanying you?"

"No. He's planning to stay here with Sema."

"Would you ask Gunnar to watch over them? He knows how much Michael means to you, so I think it would mean a lot to him."

Neo chuckled. "Have you taken up the job of Gunnar's champion?"

"It's not a job. It's a pleasure."

* * * *

Gunnar wrapped his hand around the base of Ramiro's cock as the gorgeous vampire rode up and down on his dick. There was something about the way Ramiro's muscles bunched and flexed that drove Gunnar wild. As much as he liked Michael, he couldn't imagine fucking someone so small. No. He'd come to enjoy the pleasure of holding a body as powerful as his own.

"Faster," Ramiro panted.

Gunnar began to jerk Ramiro's cock from root to tip, stopping only long enough to rub his thumb across the head before sliding back down the thick length. When Gunner caught Ramiro glance at the clock on the bedside table, his grip increased.

"Shit! Are you trying to pinch it off?" Ramiro growled.

"Just trying to get your attention back on me instead of the time." He loosened his hold and thrust up into Ramiro's ass.

"As much as my ass loves your cock, I don't think Zeus would accept us fucking as an excuse to be late."

With a roar, Gunnar grabbed Ramiro and flipped him over onto the mattress. "Then I'd better get serious about this," Gunnar said, impaling Ramiro again on his cock.

Ramiro held his legs apart as Gunnar put everything he had into fucking the man. He drove down as deep and hard as he could, hoping to telegraph his passion without having to say it. Although Ramiro was able to put his feelings into words, Gunnar preferred to convey his love by way of his actions. He hadn't grown up in a house where love was discussed, so the sentiments that came easily to others were uncomfortable to him.

"Look at me," Ramiro whispered.

Gunnar turned his attention from the point where their bodies joined to do as Ramiro asked. His thrusts slowed as he fell into the black abyss of Ramiro's gaze. Although he'd heard Ramiro's words of love, it was at that moment that he truly believed them. It was still hard to accept, but for whatever reason, Ramiro truly seemed to love him.

Gunnar's cock erupted, filling the one person he was meant to be with. As he rode out his climax, he realised not all the changes in his life were a curse. He hadn't asked to be turned into a vampire, but without his transformation he would've never given Ramiro the chance to get close to him. The change hadn't made him into an evil species. It had allowed him the common ground he needed for a life with Ramiro.

"Gunnar!" Ramiro shouted to the ceiling as he came, splashing seed between them.

With the sudden onslaught of understanding, Gunnar's chest began to ache. Trying to catch a breath, he fell to the mattress beside Ramiro.

"What's wrong?" Ramiro sat up and cupped Gunnar's face.

Gunnar couldn't speak. An overwhelming sadness descended upon him as he felt his wolf slowly retreat into the darkest depths of his soul. He could've been angry at the abandonment by his wolf, but Gunnar understood it was necessary. *Goodbye old friend.* He swallowed around the lump in his throat as oxygen once again began to move in and out of his lungs.

"He's gone," Gunnar whispered, making eye contact with Ramiro.

Ramiro's dark eyebrows drew together in apparent confusion.

"My wolf," Gunnar clarified.

Concern creased Ramiro's handsome face. "I'm sorry," he whispered, kissing Gunnar's forehead.

"It was necessary. We both knew it needed to happen for me to move on with my life." Although Gunnar would miss his wolf, he already felt more at peace with who he had become. His internal battle over, Gunnar pulled Ramiro into a deep, all-consuming kiss. He still had obstacles to overcome, but for the first time he was ready to tackle his fears head-on, as long as Ramiro was by his side.

* * * *

Shrouded in his heavy cape, Ramiro sat in the back of the gallery surrounded by demi-Gods he'd only ever read about. When the Gods entered the room,

Ramiro was forced to pull the hood lower over his face or take the risk of being burned by the sheer energy of their emanating powers.

"We are here today to decide the fate of Ian Kildare. Charged with creating a soulless species for his own gain," Zeus announced to the gathered Gods. "I have chosen Athena to question Ian Kildare. Objections?"

Ramiro had no doubt the Goddess of Wisdom would be fair, but he'd secretly hoped he would be given a chance to speak to Ian. Remembering Neo's warning, he remained silent.

When no objections were raised, Ramiro heard Athena's voice for the first time. "Bring in the accused."

Ramiro tried to block the sunlight coming from Hemera, Goddess of daylight, as he struggled to peek at Ian as he entered the room. Ian appeared indifferent to his surroundings, like being in the presence of deities was an everyday occurrence. It made Ramiro wonder how close to the surface Faelan was hiding.

"Ian Kildare, you are charged with creating the soulless creatures currently contained within County Galway, Ireland. How do you plead?" Athena began.

"Not guilty," Ian stated in a matter-of-fact tone.

"Were you not apprehended within the warded protection of the Galway pack lands?"

"Yes. I pretended to befriend the Pack Alpha, Juniper Cavanaugh, to gain entrance, nothing more," Ian stated.

"Why did you seek entrance to the pack land?"

"Because I knew Morwyn would show up eventually."

Whispered words filled the room at the mention of Morwyn. Ramiro couldn't blame the apparent unease of those around him.

"How is that possible?" Athena asked. "Morwyn has been exiled to Tartarus."

"Yes, but Juniper Cavanaugh practices the dark arts. He discovered a God can be released from Tartarus if he has a following of a thousand soulless warriors ready to follow him."

"If that were the case, Tartarus would be empty," Zeus added with a chuckle. "Blind followers are not hard to find in the world today."

"Yes, but Morwyn also holds the sickle once owned by Cronus. It was located by Cavanaugh several centuries ago."

"How do you know this?" Athena asked.

"As I've told you, I pretended to befriend Cavanaugh. Amazing what loose lips Morwyn's followers have, isn't it?" Ian crossed his arms in front of his chest and sat back in his chair with a smug smile on his face.

"Please tell the court why you failed to inform Zeus of this development earlier?" Athena continued.

"Because I knew Zeus would put an end to Juniper Cavanaugh's plans and I couldn't have that," Ian explained.

"Why is that?" Zeus butted in once again.

For the first time since entering the room, Ian shifted uncomfortably in his chair. "I planned to kill Morwyn when he surfaced once again."

"Why?" Zeus asked before Athena had the chance.

"I'm not allowed to discuss my reasons," Ian answered.

"You're not allowed? By whom?" Zeus' voice grew angry.

"It's forbidden."

"Gaia," Spiro said, getting to his feet.

Gasps filled the cavernous marble room at the announcement.

"Be seated," Athena ordered Spiro.

Spiro turned to address Zeus. "Tell them what you know."

"Remove him from the proceedings," Zeus ordered.

Neo held up his hand to hold off the demi-Gods who approached Spiro. He spoke into Spiro's ear and within seconds, Spiro was gone. "Spiro has returned to The Realm," Neo announced.

"There will be no more disruptions of these proceedings," Zeus announced.

"Calm down, you overzealous tyrant," a voice said from out of nowhere.

Zeus bowed his head. "Gaia."

Ramiro studied the room but could not tell where the voice was coming from.

"You will release Ian Kildare and give him back his sword or face Morwyn with no other way to kill him. It was the decision of many members of this court, including you, that exiled Morwyn to Tartarus instead of choosing to put an end to him all those years ago. Now is the time to right your wrong."

"Are you asking us to release Morwyn into the world on the off-chance that Ian Kildare can get close enough to kill him?" Zeus asked.

"Don't play dumb with me, Zeus!" Gaia shouted, knocking several chunks of marble loose from the ceiling. "You know exactly what I'm talking about. The time has come for you to make it right. Make it happen, or I will."

"Clear the gallery!" Zeus yelled.

Ramiro glanced at Neo, wondering if Neo would also be removed. Neo made a gesture with his head for Ramiro to leave. Ramiro wasted no time following orders. He had the feeling Olympus was about to get very loud.

* * * *

A knock at the door interrupted Spiro's telling of the events. Gunnar rose from the chair before striding towards the door of Neo's palace apartment. "Yes?" he asked through the heavily-warded door.

"It's me," Ramiro answered.

Gunnar opened the door and pulled Ramiro into his arms. He hadn't said it before Ramiro left, but Gunnar didn't like the man he loved travelling to Olympus. He'd heard nothing but bad things about the home of the Gods. "I'm glad you're back."

"It wasn't by choice," Ramiro said, kissing Gunnar.

Gunnar released Ramiro and led him to the gathering area in front of the fireplace. "What happened?"

Ramiro sat next to Gunnar on the sofa. "Gaia made an appearance. Well, her voice did, but I couldn't see her."

"You wouldn't have been able to. Only Gods have the strength to behold her image in person," Spiro explained. "What did she say?"

"Basically that she wanted Ian to kill Morwyn with the sword. She also hinted that Zeus knew."

Spiro jumped up, unsettling Sema who was resting his head in Spiro's lap. "I knew it! I told Neo I didn't trust his father. What did Zeus say to Gaia?" Spiro asked, pacing back and forth in front of the fireplace.

"Nothing much. Gaia issued Zeus the ultimatum that if he didn't take care of it she would. Then he issued the order to clear the gallery. As far as I know Neo's still there."

"Will he be okay?" Michael asked Spiro.

"Yes." Spiro resumed his seat, accepting Sema's presence in his lap once more. He gazed down into the golden eyes of the jaguar. "If only you could talk to me," he whispered.

The exchange tore at Gunnar's heart. Even before Spiro had discovered his mate was trapped inside the jaguar, there had been an obvious connection between the pair. In the last several months, rarely had Gunnar seen Spiro without Sema at his side.

"It'll be over soon," Neo announced, appearing just behind Michael. "Zeus has already begun the process to send Ian to Tartarus."

"And Ian agreed to that?" Ramiro asked.

"He had little choice after Zeus retrieved the sickle from Juniper's cabin. And since Zeus refused to allow Morwyn out of his cell, the only way for Ian to get close enough to kill him was to join him. At least Zeus has promised Ian a retrial once Morwyn is dead."

"So what now?" Spiro asked. "Did you find out why Ian needs to kill Morwyn?"

"It's the only way to break Gaia's spell that holds Faelan within Ian's body. I assume the same goes for Nialo. Zeus refused to enlighten the Gods as to why Gaia cast the spell in the first place, but I think it has something to do with Morwyn being exiled instead of put to death."

Spiro scratched Sema behind the ears. "Will you be able to tell us one day?"

Sema lifted his head and licked Spiro's chin. Whether or not Sema understood the question was anyone's guess.

The biggest question in Gunnar's mind was whether or not Nialo had truly survived intact throughout the years.

"What about the hybrids? What happens to them?" Ramiro asked.

"They've already been destroyed. Well, all of them with the exception of Juniper. Galena asked for him to be caged for a while before his execution," Neo explained. "The Galway pack lands are being awarded to Galena and Flick who have decided to stay in Ireland." Neo moved around the chair and picked Michael up before depositing the smaller man on his lap.

"Haig ought to be happy about that," Gunnar remarked.

"Yes, he is. He's actually planning to take Kern and Audric with him to help Galena rebuild their village."

"Haig and Kern quit?" Both weres were damn good guards, but more than that, they were Gunnar's friends.

"Not for good. Just long enough to help Galena get back on her feet. I told them their job at the vineyard would be waiting for them when they were ready." Neo kissed the side of Michael's head. "You ready to go home, baby?"

Michael started to nod, but stopped after the first dip of his head. "What about Sema? Can we leave him here?"

Neo turned his attention to Sema. "I have a feeling this is where he belongs."

"You're right," Spiro agreed. "Whether it takes Ian an hour or a decade to kill Morwyn, I want to be with Nialo when the spell is broken."

Gunnar noticed the unspoken exchange between Michael and Neo. Evidently Gunnar wasn't the only one worried about Nialo's mental or physical health once he was released. Gunnar stared at the big black jaguar. Even knowing a God was inside Sema, Gunnar felt a great deal of sadness that his old friend would most likely cease to exist once Nialo emerged. Sema had become part of the landscape at the vineyard. What would it be like without him around, sunning himself on the patio or following Neo up and down the rows of grapes?

Ramiro chose that moment to squeeze Gunnar's hand, reminding him that he wouldn't be alone once they returned to Le uve del Regno. He smiled at the man he loved. Spiro deserved the kind of love Gunnar had found even if it meant saying goodbye to his old friend Sema.

Epilogue

"You wanted to see me?" Gunnar asked, stepping into the familiar office.

"Have a seat." Neo gestured to the wingback chair beside him.

Since returning to the vineyard the week before, Neo had been splitting his time between home and The Realm. Gunnar knew Spiro was in a state of extreme irritation as he continued to count the days until the battle between Ian and Morwyn ended. Neo had had little choice but to step in and help his brother with the running of The Realm. Although Gunnar understood, it had left him on edge.

"I have something for you." Neo dug into his suit jacket pocket and retrieved a business-sized envelope before passing it to Gunnar. "I know we haven't had a chance to talk about the future, but I wanted to make sure you got this before I'm called away again."

Gunnar prayed for good news as he carefully opened the envelope. It contained a single sheet of paper, a deed by the look of it. "What's this?"

"Ramiro told me you had your eyes on a spot of land in the woods. That's the deed. It's yours to do with what you want."

Gunnar couldn't believe it. "Thank you."

Neo leant forward, resting his forearms on his knees. "Don't thank me. It's a bribe of sorts."

"A bribe?"

"I hope by giving you that piece of land you'll stick around even though I've been a complete ass lately. I need you to know I can't imagine trusting Michael's safety with anyone but you in charge."

Gunnar was overwhelmed by the gesture. He cleared his throat. "I'm a vampire now. What if the men don't respect me enough to listen to me?"

"Then fire them, but I doubt that's the case. They didn't follow you because you were a werewolf. They followed you because you're a natural-born leader. That hasn't changed. Believe me, it took me a hell of a long time to come to grips with what happened to me. It was Michael who finally taught me to accept who I'd become."

"As Ramiro has done for me," Gunnar acknowledged.

"Yes. We will need to make a few changes, however. You're still too young to function during the daylight hours, so I would like to put Haig as your second in charge."

"Haig would be my choice, as well. What about Ramiro? Will you allow him to live here with me and still keep his security position for the vampire species?"

"Of course. As long as you understand there will be times when he'll be called away on business." Neo sat back and reached for a glass of Liquid Crimson. "Would you care for a glass?"

"No, thank you. I've promised Ramiro we'd go into town for dinner."

Neo grinned. "Have you grown to enjoy the taste of human blood from the source?"

Embarrassed that he'd refused for so long, Gunnar nodded. "It was never the blood I had a problem with. More like the way it was obtained, but Ramiro and I've worked out a good system."

"I won't keep you then. I have a dinner date myself waiting for me." Neo emptied his wine glass before following Gunnar out of the office. "Perhaps once things settle down we'll have a chance to go fishing."

"You don't fish," Gunnar reminded Neo.

"No, I don't, but I'd welcome an evening spent with an old friend."

Gunnar left the house with his future in his hand and warmth in his heart.

* * * *

Ramiro felt the hard length of Gunnar's erection as it pressed against his hip. "What about that one? He looks like he could handle both of us," he suggested.

"You think he's into guys?" Gunnar asked, fishing Ramiro's cock out of his pants.

"By the way he's watching us, I'd say his answer is a big 'hell yeah'." Ramiro smiled at the muscular man across the room, giving him the signal to approach.

The man wasted no time making his way through the crowd. "Hey."

"Hey, yourself," Ramiro returned, eyeing the man up and down. It wasn't easy to find a donor large enough to feed two vampires at the same time, but occasionally they got lucky. "What's your name?"

"Alec," the man said, his eyes on Ramiro's cock.

Ramiro glanced down and watched Gunnar manipulate his erection for several moments before returning his attention to the menu. "Think you can handle both of us?"

Alec's Adams apple bobbed several times before he answered. "I've never done two at a time, but I'd sure as hell like to try."

"We hoped you'd say that." Gunnar released Ramiro's cock and motioned to the back corner of the bar. "Let's head over there out of the way."

Ramiro rolled his eyes and whispered in Alec's ear. "Gunnar's still a little shy."

Alec moaned when Ramiro's lips caressed his ear. "That's okay."

Once they reached the corner, Ramiro pressed himself against Alec's back as Gunnar pulled Alec against his chest. Sandwiched between the two vampires, Alec's heart began to pound loud enough for Ramiro to hear. Gods he loved that sound. Their work was half done before they even really touched the man.

Again, Ramiro whispered in Alec's ear. "I'm going to jack you off while my friend and I kiss. Is that acceptable?"

Alec nodded, moving to quickly unzip his jeans.

Ramiro stared into Gunnar's eyes. "Make his blood sweet as candy," he instructed Gunnar.

Gunnar grunted before leaning his head over Alec's shoulder to capture Ramiro's mouth in an erotic game of tongue play.

Ramiro flicked his tongue in and out of Gunnar's mouth, teasing the man he loved. He'd offered to jack their chosen donor, but Gunnar had refused. According to Gunnar, the only way he felt in control of the situation was if he did the required touching.

Since it hadn't mattered either way to Ramiro, he gave in without a fuss.

Gunnar grunted again, and shook his head when Ramiro mentally plunged a finger into his lover's hole. Gunnar broke the kiss. "Not here. He's almost done."

By the sound of Alec's beating heart, Ramiro knew Gunnar was right. Only once had they lost themselves enough to fuck in the bar, and it hadn't ended well. Gunnar was still too possessive to allow anyone to witness their lovemaking. Ramiro had no doubt Gunnar would eventually change his mind, but he knew baby steps were required. Allowing Gunnar to reach the conclusion that all vampires reached eventually needed to be at his own pace.

Soon, hopefully, Gunnar would see the beauty in watching and being watched, but until then, Ramiro would happily take the two of them home to bed after dinner. He felt Alec's body began to buck, obviously on the verge of climax. "Dinner time," he whispered to Gunnar.

Gunnar's fangs slid from their sheathes. Ramiro watched Gunnar sink his teeth into Alec's neck before moving to the other side to enjoy his meal. He felt Gunnar's free hand knead his ass and Ramiro let his eyes drift shut.

Everything was better with Gunnar. Life had taken on a completely new dimension for Ramiro since he'd found the love of the strong Alpha. He let out a sigh, content with the knowledge that he'd never again have to walk the Earth alone.

ROYAL BLOOD

Dedication

Thanks to all of you have waited patiently for the final story in the Neo's Realm series. Although this book was a long time coming, I'm thrilled with the result. I hope you all enjoy reading it as much as I enjoyed writing it.

Chapter One

Spiro Manos stared at the large black jaguar asleep next to him. It had been four months since he'd learnt Nialo, the mate chosen for him by the Gods, was trapped inside the body of his brother's pet, Sema. He reached out and ran his fingers through Sema's thick fur. He couldn't reconcile the fact that the black jaguar was his promised mate Nialo. At least while Nialo was still in cat form, it was easier for Spiro to think of the jaguar as Sema.

Sema lifted his head and yawned before moving closer to Spiro's side.

Spiro smiled and waited for the big cat to drift back to sleep before allowing his emotions to rise to the surface. An entire realm of Blessed Creatures believed in his ability to heal them through wisdom and magic, but where were those powers when he needed them the most?

He felt Sema's deep, rumbling purr against his chest, breaking his heart even more. As hard as it had been for him to live a life knowing he'd never have a chance to be with the one being meant for him, Nialo had been trapped inside an animal. What Spiro didn't understand was how Sema had suffered for centuries in silence without becoming feral.

"Can you understand me?" he whispered.

Sema opened his eyes once again and raised enough to rub his head against Spiro's chin. *Was that a yes?* Spiro wondered. A large part of him hoped Nialo could hear and understand what he said, but that would mean Nialo's suffering over the centuries had been even greater.

Spiro sighed and rested his forehead against the jaguar. "I don't know how you've done it for so long. Barely four months and I'm starting to feel off kilter. Should I speak to Sema or Nialo? Which one do you consider yourself?"

The jaguar moved to nuzzle Spiro's groin through the blanket. It was an action Sema would have never attempted. "Shit!" Spiro shouted in surprise. "Enough of that." He gently nudged Sema's head away from his cock. "Although, I guess, that answers my question."

Still rattled by the nuzzling and his body's reaction, Spiro crawled out of bed. He turned his back to Sema and pulled on a pair of silk pyjama bottoms along with his matching robe to hide his hard cock. His entire adult life he'd slept in the nude, but perhaps he needed to rethink his choice of attire around Sema, at least until Ian Kildare, the King of the Vampires, had successfully completed his mission to kill Morwyn and reverse the spell Gaia had cast on Nialo.

Spiro groaned. Even the thought of seeing Nialo face to face was enough to harden his cock even further. He glanced over his shoulder. "Stay here," he ordered Sema before leaving the bedroom.

He made his way through the candlelit halls to the staircase. He took the stairs two at a time and within moments he was in the library and heading down the narrow passage. Once inside the vault, Spiro shut the door, something he rarely did, and went to the backroom where the portraits were safely stored.

He didn't even need to think about which drawer he was interested in. Although the other drawers of paintings were filed chronologically, the one he was after had been organised by Neo with Spiro in mind. It was just one more reason he loved his brother.

Spiro opened the large, thin drawer and under the soft glow of the specialised lighting, he gazed at his favourite portrait of Nialo. It had been painted soon after Morwyn had taken a sword and separated himself from his conjoined twin, Nialo.

He retrieved a small stool from the end of the row of cabinets and carried it over to sit on. There had been days when a simple glimpse of Nialo's likeness was enough to satisfy him, but not anymore. Spiro held his fingers over the aged canvas. He longed to touch the image of the handsome man with sorrowful eyes that stared up at him.

Although the depiction clearly showed a lot of Nialo's muscular physique, it was the eyes that always held Spiro captive. Despite Nialo's bronze-coloured skin and black hair, the eyes were the brightest blue he'd ever seen. Spiro had fallen in love with those eyes before his eighteenth birthday and his feelings had only grown stronger over the centuries.

"Thought I might find you here," Neo said.

Spiro jumped and spun around, nearly falling off the stool. "The vault's door was shut for a reason."

Neo walked across the room and looked down at the painting. Hands in pockets, Neo shook his head. "I can't believe you're still doing this to yourself."

"Doing what, looking at the man I love?"

"He's not a man, brother. That's the one thing you always failed to understand," Neo began.

"I know what he is." Spiro stared down at the canvas. He couldn't tell his brother he'd had dreams of being fucked by the perfect being in the portrait for so long he couldn't reconcile Nialo's God status.

Spiro glanced back up at Neo. "Did you need something?"

Neo moved to lean against the cabinet. "There's something bugging me that I need to talk to you about."

"Okay." Spiro waited for his brother to continue. It was Neo's obvious unease that made Spiro nervous. "What's going on?"

Neo ran a hand through his hair. "Just something Zeus said in passing that's been bugging me since."

Spiro stood and closed the drawer, shutting Nialo's portrait away from the upcoming conversation. "What did he say?"

"It wasn't what he came right out and said." Neo sighed. "You know how he is. He just mumbled something about convincing the Gods that Nialo deserved a mate in his memory."

"What's that supposed to mean?"

Neo ran his fingers through his hair. "I think you were never meant to be Nialo's Divine mate. When Zeus deemed the two of you bonded, Nialo was already lost to this world, or so everyone believed. If that's what really happened, it breaks my heart that Zeus would knowingly bind your spirit to Nialo, knowing you would have a lonely existence."

"I don't understand why that would surprise you. Zeus has never liked me. Despite the sorrow he might display to everyone else, I think he knew exactly what he'd be doing to me by creating the bond."

Neo slid open the door and glanced down at the portrait. "I hope you're wrong. I'd have to try and kill my own father for doing something so cold-hearted."

Spiro reached out and touched Neo's forearm. "It would be suicide to go up against Zeus."

"Yes, but I've no doubt I'd try."

As strong as Neo was it would end in a bloodbath for his brother if he dared go up against his father. Spiro needed to diffuse the situation before Neo's anger got the better of him. "Well, if that was Zeus' plan I can't wait to see the look on his face once the spell is broken and Nialo and I can be together. Besides, if anyone has the power to go up against Zeus it will be Nialo."

Neo looked down at the portrait again. He continued to stare at it for several moments before he let out a sigh. "When I rescued Sema, he'd been forced to live in a small cage with barely enough room in which to turn around. He had wounds old and new from his master's whip. When I confronted the master, he explained Sema had been passed down from generation to generation. He hated being the eldest son stuck with the responsibility of looking after the cat."

Neo glanced up to meet Spiro's gaze. "That man was the first human I killed out of anger. The guilt of realising the monster I'd become drove me to Le uve del Regno. I showered Sema with love and affection, hoping to undo the damage the man had caused."

"And you did," Spiro cut in.

"Yes," Neo agreed. "But I thought he was simply a magical pet. When in reality he's my uncle." Neo shook his head. "I still haven't wrapped my mind around it."

"Me either." Spiro debated over how much to tell Neo for several seconds before coming to a decision. "I don't know if it was the bite inflicted by Ramiro or something else, but Nialo is very much present in Sema."

"How do you know? Have you been able to communicate with him?"

Spiro felt his face heat in embarrassment. "I asked earlier this evening. Sema answered by nuzzling my...balls. He's never done that before, which leads me to believe Nialo is presently in control of Sema's body."

Neo began to chuckle, softly at first, but it soon turned into an all-out belly laugh. "Oh, Brother, I wish I could've seen your face when that happened."

"It's not funny." Spiro wasn't about to admit to his brother that Sema's attention had made him hard as a rock.

"Maybe not to you, but I think it's hilarious. Next thing you know Sema will mount you while you sleep."

Spiro slammed the door shut, hiding the portrait from his view. He stood and adjusted his robe. "If you're finished, I'm going back to bed."

Neo wiped the moisture, caused by his laughter, from his eyes. "I'm sorry. I shouldn't have reacted that way. I know how hard this is for you."

Spiro's thoughts went back to his body's reaction earlier. "You have no idea."

"You're right, but maybe Ramiro does. Have you talked to him? After all, he was inside Nialo's mind.

He might be able to shed some light on the situation for you."

Spiro hadn't sought out Ramiro's advice, partly because he was afraid of the answers he might receive. "I'll think about it."

* * * *

Nialo sat in the centre of Spiro's bed like he'd been instructed. It had taken all his strength not to defy Spiro's orders and go after his mate, especially after he'd witnessed the way Spiro's body had reacted to his attentions.

When Gaia had first changed him into a jaguar, Nialo had nearly gone insane. Despite his mother's calming words that it was for the best, Nialo had hated her. He'd used what little power he'd had left to hide himself from Gaia and run away.

Alone in the world, Nialo had been lucky enough to happen upon a farmer taking a midday nap at the edge of his field. With wolves in the area, Nialo had worried for the lone man and had curled up beside the farmer to watch over him. Just as he'd predicted, the wolves had caught scent of the man and had come to investigate.

When the wolves had entered the clearing, Nialo had sat up and roared for the first time since being changed. The sound had woken the farmer, who had immediately tried to back away from Nialo only to find himself quickly confronted with the small pack of wolves.

Taking a chance, Nialo had insinuated himself between the man and the hungry wolves. Outnumbered five to one, the ensuing fight had been a bloody one, but once over, Nialo had killed four of the wolves and had run off the fifth. Nialo had been badly injured, but the kind farmer had picked him up and carried him back to his small home in the woods.

It had been the years spent with the man and his family that had convinced Nialo it would be better to forget his previous self and learn to adapt to life as a jaguar. During the centuries that followed, a series of members of the farmer's family had been assigned the task of taking care of their fierce and loyal protector.

It had been spending time with Spiro that had begun to pull Nialo out of his animal state. The overwhelming need to stay close to Spiro had progressed steadily until it had come to a head a few months earlier when Nialo had prodded Ramiro into biting him. There were still memories trapped within his own mind, but he knew they would surface eventually. For now, it was Spiro he was concerned about.

Now that the truth was known, Nialo's need for Spiro only increased. He watched his Divine mate suffer through the confusion the truth had uncovered and wanted to offer comfort. Nialo longed to wrap Spiro in his arms and kiss away the tears that fell too frequently.

Nialo stretched before jumping to the floor. The jaguar left the bedroom determined to find Spiro and lead him back to bed.

* * * *

Spiro stood outside Ramiro's new house at the vineyard, his hand poised to knock. When he heard the unmistakeable sounds of sex going on inside, he dropped his hand and took a step back. Intruding on a private moment wasn't what he'd had in mind.

Gunnar and Ramiro were still in the honeymoon phase of their relationship, so Spiro knew the two of them would probably go for hours without taking a break. The thought brought Spiro's cock to attention. He reached down to press a hand against his aroused member and realised he was still in his robe. "Dammit."

Closing his eyes, Spiro mumbled a short chant. His body began to tingle as the magic easily dressed him in a pair of loose-fitting white linen pants and matching shirt. Although many in The Realm felt comfortable in jeans, they were far too constricting for Spiro's taste. He preferred the subtle brush of cloth against his unencumbered cock to the tight confines of heavy denim.

Spiro thought about waiting for Gunnar and Ramiro to finish their lovemaking, but decided his time was better spent in The Realm. He shook his head. No, it wasn't The Realm he needed to get back to, it was Nialo.

He'd barely begun the chant that would take him home when the front door opened.

"I thought I smelled you out here," Gunnar said, standing naked in the doorway.

"I didn't mean to...interrupt."

"You didn't." Gunnar grinned. "Ramiro's a lot older than I am, it'll take him a few minutes to recover sufficiently to go again." He stepped back and waved Spiro inside. "Is everything okay?"

Spiro shook his head and entered the cabin. "I was hoping to speak with Ramiro." It took everything he had to keep his gaze from drifting to Gunnar's impressive lower-half.

"Spiro," Ramiro greeted, coming into the room. He tossed Gunnar a pair of sweats and rolled his eyes. "Please forgive my mate's lack of modesty."

Gunnar laughed and pulled on the pants. "Never heard you complain about seeing me naked," he told Ramiro.

Ramiro ignored Gunnar and motioned Spiro over to the couch. "You look troubled."

Spiro sat on the edge of the sofa, wondering how much he should reveal. Neo had been right about one thing. Ramiro was the only one who had been given a glimpse inside Nialo's head. "I need to talk to you about Nialo."

"I had a feeling you'd get around to asking when you were ready. What do you want to know?" Ramiro asked.

Before Spiro could speak, Gunnar cleared his throat. "While the two of you are talking, I'm gonna hop in the shower."

Spiro waited for Gunnar to kiss Ramiro and leave the room before continuing. "I believe that Nialo is fully present within Sema, and I guess I just need confirmation."

Ramiro rubbed his palms together in thought. "Yes and no. Yes, Nialo is fully present, but he's not inside of Sema. He is Sema. Unlike a were, Nialo was transformed into Sema. There is no one trapped inside the other. You would do well to think of the jaguar as only Nialo. Sema is simply a name given to his changed form, but it's not his true name. Does that make sense?"

Spiro thought of the embarrassing sexual attention Nialo had given him earlier. "It makes sense, but I can't allow myself to see a jaguar as the mate I've longed for all my life. It's not natural."

"None of this is natural. Don't beat yourself up over something you have no control over. Your mind may tell you Nialo is a jaguar, but it would only be natural for your body to respond to your mate."

Spiro straightened as he remembered his physical reaction to the feel of Nialo's attention. "I can't allow my body to make decisions for me."

Ramiro shrugged. "I understand that. I'm just trying to tell you it would be natural for your body to be pulled in that direction. There should be no shame in what your instincts are telling you to do."

"No," Spiro said with a sharp shake of his head. He decided to change the subject. "Have you felt anything from Ian Kildare?"

"Nothing," Ramiro admitted.

Spiro ran his fingers through his long white hair. "Do you know whether or not Nialo can sense Morwyn? Maybe the link between them would be stronger."

"No. Their link was severed when Morwyn separated himself from Nialo."

Frustrated, Spiro stood and began pacing. "What's taking so long? Ian should've located and done away with Morwyn by now."

"I'm sorry. Perhaps time's different down there," Ramiro offered.

Spiro had a wealth of magic at his disposal. Surely there was something he could do. He paused in his pacing and turned to face Ramiro. "Do you think Gaia would help me?"

"I think it would be suicide for you to contact her directly."

Spiro's chest tightened as he realised what he must do. "My father might be willing to help. I'm sure Gaia would speak to him."

Ramiro's eyebrows rose. "I didn't think you had a relationship with Eros."

"I don't. Despite his attempts throughout the centuries to see me, my mother always warned me to stay away from him. But maybe it's time I paid him a visit."

"They say to look upon Eros is to fall in love," Ramiro reminded him.

"Yes, but I have little choice if I want to get to Gaia."

* * * *

Spiro was surprised to find his bedroom empty. "Nialo?" He stepped into the hall and walked to the head of the magnificent staircase. "Nialo?" he called again.

He heard the heavy tread of the large jaguar's paws as they thumped against the marble floors in an all-out run. Seconds later, Nialo appeared, leaping over four steps at a time to reach the top.

Spiro stepped back, giving Nialo room to come to a stop without bowling Spiro over in the process. The black cat balanced on his back legs as his front paws came to rest on Spiro's shoulders. Spiro turned his head as Nialo rubbed his head against Spiro's cheek. "Yes, I missed you, too," Spiro acknowledged, running his fingers through Nialo's thick pelt.

As earlier, Spiro's body took notice of Nialo's presence in a very embarrassing way. He pushed Nialo until the cat, once again, stood on four legs. "Come. I have something to discuss with you."

He led Nialo into the bedroom and shut the door. "I'm going to see my father, and I want you to come with me. I need Eros' help to contact your mother."

Nialo headbutted Spiro until he was backed against the door. Spiro reached down to try to soothe the agitated jaguar. "Is it seeing my father that you don't approve of or contacting your mother?"

Nialo roared and pressed his body against Spiro's legs. In all the years Spiro had known the jaguar, never had he heard such an angry sound come from the normally gentle cat. Spiro leaned over and wrapped his arms around Nialo's neck. "It'll be okay. I'm afraid, too, but I have to know if there's something I can do to help King Kildare defeat Morwyn."

Nialo moved enough to give Spiro some room. He fell to his knees and buried his face in the soft black fur. "I need you. I want to feel your arms around me, and I can't have that until this spell is broken."

Nialo settled quickly upon hearing Spiro's plea.

Spiro kissed the top of Nialo's head. "Thank you."

* * * *

The pale yellow palace was more beautiful than Spiro had imagined. No wonder Eros chose to seclude himself in such surroundings. Spiro reached down and rubbed Nialo's back. He'd need the unspoken strength of his mate to get through his first meeting with his father. Although he often made jokes about Neo's father, at least Zeus could be addressed without the fear of falling under his spell. Not that Neo cared to talk to Zeus unless absolutely necessary, but the option had at least been there.

Perhaps if Spiro concentrated on Nialo instead of Eros he could escape the lure of his father's beauty. "Stay close," he whispered to Nialo as they neared the massive front door. Before he could knock, the door swung open with the help of a heavily muscled man.

"Eros is waiting for you," the man announced. He glanced down at Nialo. "No pets."

Spiro narrowed his eyes. With one incantation, he could make the man forever flaccid. "Hold your tongue or regret it," he seethed.

The man was intelligent enough to step back without another word. He gestured towards the back of the palace before disappearing into an adjoining room.

Nialo rubbed his head against Spiro's hip.

"Don't worry," Spiro whispered. He gave Nialo's head several loving strokes before proceeding farther.

The grand hall opened onto an interior courtyard, overflowing with a profusion of exotic plants and flowers. In the centre was a large velvet tufted piece of furniture that was obviously used for more than just sleeping. His grip on the scruff of Nialo's neck tightened at the first glimpse of Eros.

Surrounded by naked men and women, Eros' attention was squarely on Spiro. "At long last, my son has finally come to meet me."

Spiro gestured towards the mass of devoted love slaves. "Can we talk without an audience?"

With a flick of his hand, Eros sent everyone scurrying back into the shadowed halls leading off the courtyard. "Satisfied?"

Spiro looked down at Nialo. Now that he was in front of Eros, he felt he owed his father more than he'd prepared himself to give. He found a marble bench and settled with Nialo beside him. "I know I should have made the effort earlier, but my mother warned me to keep my distance."

"Look at me," Eros commanded.

"I can't. I know what will happen."

"No you don't. Look. At. Me."

Nialo prodded Spiro's arm with his head. It was a leap of faith to believe Eros. He took a deep breath before looking up to address his father. He blew out the breath he had held tight in his chest. *Nothing.* Although Eros was truly the most beautiful man Nialo had ever seen, that's where his feelings stopped. "Mother was wrong," he mumbled in confusion.

"Not exactly. People see me the way they want to see me, and for most, they need to see love in my eyes. You don't need anything from me."

"You're wrong," Spiro admitted. "I needed a father after my mother's death."

"And I called to you, but you weren't ready to believe in me." Eros moved to a sitting position.

Spiro felt a moment's shame at his reason for finally visiting his father's palace. He lowered his chin while he searched for something to say.

"Nialo, come here," Eros called.

Spiro's head jerked up. "You know?"

"I feel love like others feel the breeze upon their skin. The moment you walked into the palace the connection between the two of you threatened to overwhelm my senses. Your bond goes beyond those of most Devine mates. But, of course, Nialo is not a demi-god is he?"

Nialo jumped up on the tufted platform and presented himself. Eros placed a hand on the top of Nialo's head and stared into the jaguar's eyes. He immediately pulled his hand away as if he'd been burnt and broke eye contact.

Turning away, Eros looked at Spiro with tears in his eyes. "He's too powerful. Zeus was wrong to bind the two of you."

Spiro felt like he'd been slapped. Whether or not Zeus had made a mistake, Nialo was his mate, and the two of them would be bound until their last breath. "Zeus didn't even know Nialo was still alive. From what Neo told me, it was Zeus' idea of honouring Nialo."

Eros shook his head. "Lost is not the same as dead, and Zeus wouldn't make that kind of mistake."

"What're you saying?"

Eros rose, stopping only long enough to wrap a sheet around his waist before walking over to sit beside Spiro. "If Gaia's spell is broken, Nialo will be too much for you to handle." He put a hand on Spiro's shoulder. "I know you love him, and I know your mother taught you well in the arts of magic, but they won't be enough."

Anger boiled up inside Spiro. Mumbling under his breath, he reached up and removed Eros' hand from his shoulder, sending a bolt of electricity through his father's body. Eros crumpled to the ground, his eyes rounded in a combination of pain and surprise.

Spiro stood and looked down at Eros. "Nialo and I have suffered enough, and I'm not about to let you or anyone else keep us apart. Fuck Zeus, and fuck you." He strode towards the hallway. "Nialo!"

Within seconds the black jaguar was at Spiro's side as they left the pale yellow palace.

Chapter Two

Nialo sat at Spiro's side as the meeting continued. Unlike past meetings, Nialo was fully engaged in what was being said. He wanted so much to be part of the conversation.

"It's just a setback," Ramiro argued. "Ian's not dead."

"Yet," Neo added, "Kildare may have the heart to destroy Morwyn, but not the strength or the magic."

Nialo opened his mouth to tell them what he knew, but the only sound he made was a frustrated roar. He sprang to his feet and began pacing the room. There had to be a way for Gaia to break the spell without sending Ian—Faelen—to his death.

Nialo scratched at the door, carving deep grooves into the heavy wood.

"What's wrong?" Spiro asked, kneeling beside Nialo.

Despite his anger at the situation, Nialo calmed at Spiro's touch. He stared into the silvery eyes that said more than words ever could. The conversation Spiro had had with Eros still weighed heavily on Nialo's mind. Although Spiro didn't want to hear the truth spilling from Eros' lips, Nialo did.

After rubbing his cheek against Spiro's, Nialo scratched at the door once again, hoping to get his point across. He knew Spiro wouldn't understand, but he prayed his mate would believe in him enough to open the door.

Several seconds ticked by before Spiro stood and opened the door. Nialo looked up, willing Spiro to believe in him. There was only one way to kill Morwyn, and Nialo was the only one who could get it done.

With one last look at Spiro, Nialo slipped into the hall.

* * * *

Getting inside the pale yellow palace was easy. Nialo jumped through an open window and crept towards the stairs. His nose told him Eros was in his bedchamber entertaining. Careful not to draw attention, the jaguar waited in the shadowed hall until he was sure no one would see him. He ran up the steps and straight to the door that smelt like Eros.

From their earlier connection, Nialo knew Eros was already aware of his presence. He sat outside the bedroom door and waited. Within seconds the door opened and a nude man and woman left the room.

"Come in," Eros called.

Nialo walked into the room and jumped onto the wide bench at the foot of Eros' bed. He stared into the bright eyes of the naked man and waited for the connection to begin.

"I'm not surprised you came back." Eros readjusted his pillows before leaning back against the headboard.

"Why don't I have the ability to communicate with Spiro like I can you?" he asked without spoken words.

"My son is a demi-god. The fae half of him blocks the transmission. It would simply be too much for his body to handle."

"If that's the case, why can't I speak to Gaia?" Nialo asked.

"She's not in The Realm. Gaia hasn't lived among people or gods of any kind for several millennia. I'll send you there, but I can't guarantee she'll be pleased."

"The legend on how to kill my brother is wrong, and Gaia knows it. I'm locked in this body, and only my mother has the power to reverse the spell."

"So why hasn't she done so before now?" Eros asked.

"Because she knew I wasn't ready to go against Morwyn."

"And you are now?"

Nialo thought about killing his brother. Despite everything, he still loved Morwyn. Still, there was someone he loved even more. *"Spiro needs me. And the thought of Morwyn harming him in any way is reason enough to put an end to all of this."*

Eros nodded. "That is a fear I've lived with since Zeus proclaimed my son as your Devine mate. I, too, will be glad to see the threat to Spiro eliminated."

"Then send me to Gaia."

* * * *

Disgusted, Spiro threw the ancient text across his workroom. "It's useless!"

Michael picked up the book and gently set it on Spiro's workbench. "Neo won't stop looking for Nialo until he's found."

Spiro gathered his hair and began to braid it into one long strand that would hang down the centre of his back. He'd felt the emptiness of Nialo's departure the moment he'd stepped foot out of The Realm. "He's no longer in The Realm." He rubbed his chest. "It's as if a black hole has found its way into my body where my heart should be."

Michael wrapped strong arms around Spiro's waist and hugged him. "Where could he have gone? Would he be welcomed on Olympus?"

"Of course. But I can't feel him at all." Spiro closed his eyes and kissed Michael's forehead. "I need to get back to work. There's got to be a way to find him."

Michael gave Spiro another hug before stepping back. "I'm here if you need me."

"I know." Spiro brushed Michael's cheek with his palm. "I love you."

"Love you, too, Dad."

As much as he loved his surrogate son, Spiro needed to concentrate. He'd spent the majority of his life counselling others but talking about his own feelings wasn't as easy. What if Nialo didn't return? Spiro couldn't help but remember what Eros had said. Maybe Nialo knew the truth behind the warning and had left before Eros' prediction could come true?

After the door shut behind Michael, Spiro returned to the wall of books. He scanned the spines, looking for answers, something he could use to connect with Nialo. As he studied the available tomes, tears filled his eyes, making it difficult to read.

With the old leather-bound book clutched to his chest, Spiro climbed onto the bed he kept in his workshop. He rested his head on a pillow and closed his eyes. Although he thought of his mother often, rarely had he needed her as much as he did at that moment.

* * * *

Nialo sat at the base of the barren mountain. Not one tree, blade of grass or other sign of life could be seen. Did his mother really hate all living things to the point that she'd separate herself to such a degree?

The climb wouldn't be an easy one. Few would have been able to make it at all, but the particular gifts that came along with his jaguar body would give him an advantage. He studied the craggy grey rocks for several moments before starting his ascent.

After two hours of climbing, Nialo was only halfway up the mountain and the terrain was getting steeper. He found a narrow ledge and sat to gather his strength. As he looked out over the barren landscape in the distance, guilt began to settle in. What had happened to his mother to drive her to such a desolate place?

"It's what I deserve."

Nialo stood and looked around for his mother, but he was alone. *"Let me see you."*

"Why are you here? No one comes to my mountain."

"I need to talk to you. I'm ready to face Morwyn, but I can't do it in this body."

"Why now? What's changed that suddenly you are ready to do what should've been done long ago?"

Nialo wondered if he should mention his desire to be with Spiro the way a mate should be. *"Because I know killing Morwyn is the only way to ensure Spiro's safety."*

Gaia made a disapproving noise. "Zeus should have never bound the two of you. It was pure selfishness on his part. Unfortunately, I cannot undo what he's done."

"I don't care why Zeus did it. I love Spiro, and I want to keep him safe." He wondered what selfishness Gaia was referring to. As far as he knew, Zeus had bound him to Spiro as a gesture of honour.

When no answer came from Gaia, Nialo started to worry. *"Please."*

"You need to be sure. Tartarus is a very unforgiving place. Even if you succeed and make it out alive, your soul will forever carry part of the darkness of Tartarus. If you go up against Morwyn you must be prepared to end this. I will give you five days. On the morning of the sixth day if your brother still lives, I will pull you back to The Realm, and you will reclaim your animal skin forever."

Five days. Nialo wasn't arrogant. He knew he could be in for a long bloody battle with his twin, but the chance to hold Spiro in his arms forever was worth risking everything for. *"And Ian Kildare? Will he be allowed to return to The Realm?"*

"Ian is out of his depth with Morwyn. He hides like a child," Gaia spat.

Nialo knew how powerful Ian was. He wondered if Gaia's punishment of transforming Faelen into Ian Kildare had something to do with it. If the King of the Fae hid like a child, Nialo had to wonder what kind of power Morwyn had at his disposal. *"Then why did you tell Zeus to send him to kill Morwyn?"*

"I hoped Faelen's powers would emerge once he was in Tartarus. Sacrificing you was not an option," Gaia replied.

"So why now?"

"Your inability to truly be with your mate is already killing you. It might be just the motivation you need to finally stand up for yourself against your brother."

Nialo hated the pity in his mother's voice, but he had no doubt she was telling the truth. Loving without being able to touch or speak to Spiro had been weighing heavily on his heart. *"Give me an extra day so that I might explain this to Spiro and truly feel the love that I may never feel again."*

"You ask for too much," Gaia said.

Nialo growled in anger. He knew he risked everything by going against his mother, but he'd waited centuries for a single kiss from his mate. *"I ask for what I am owed. Give me one day to live a lifetime with Spiro before I face my brother."*

Gaia was silent for several moments. "Your powers feed off your brother's. Although Morwyn is in Tartarus, your powers will be amplified while he still draws breath. It was the way you were created. Together you and Morwyn are unstoppable, and that did not change once Morwyn separated the two of you. Your power and hidden anger have grown too great for The Realm. A single touch from you would certainly kill anyone in your path, including your mate. There is a way…"

"Tell me," Nialo pleaded.

"I can protect your mate as I did you while you are in The Realm," Gaia proclaimed.

Nialo hated the thought of condemning Spiro to the same fate he'd lived with, but he owed Spiro and his friends the truth. Unfortunately, the only way he could communicate while still keeping Spiro safe, was to see his mate turned into an animal. *"Only until I travel to Tartarus,"* he demanded.

"I am doing you a great favour. Do not push me," Gaia answered.

"I am your son, and I am pleading with you," Nialo implored.

"Fine, but you will only have the safety of twenty-four hours. It would be wise for you to remember that."

* * * *

Spiro awoke to the sound of the bedroom door opening. He sat up expecting to see his beloved jaguar, and realised there was something wrong. Spiro's body moved differently than he was used to. Looking down, he began to panic as he discovered white fur where his pale skin should have been. Spiro opened his mouth and sounded a loud roar.

"It's okay, love. You'll return to normal soon," a deep voice said.

Spiro turned his attention to the nude man in the doorway. Although his nose and heart knew the man was his mate, Spiro couldn't believe his eyes. He'd seen portraits of Nialo, but the painter had to have been visually impaired. As beautiful as he thought the image of Nialo was, it didn't hold a candle to the real thing. He jumped off the bed and crashed to the floor in an ungraceful heap of fur.

"Easy," Nialo said, sitting on the floor beside Spiro, his voice scratchy from underuse. "It'll take a few moments to get comfortable in your new form."

Spiro couldn't help but purr as Nialo began to stroke his head.

"I need you to listen to me," Nialo soothed. "This is the only way the two of us can be together until I kill Morwyn."

Spiro sat up and roared his displeasure at the thought of Nialo going up against Morwyn.

"It's the only way. I'm the only one who has the power to take on Morwyn and have a chance of winning. We need to find Neo. There is much to explain and only a short time to do it." Nialo leant down and kissed the top of Spiro's head. "I wanted a chance to tell you how much I love you. It pains me that we can't be together the way we both want right now, but my powers would kill you with one touch. Gaia promised to turn you back after I leave."

Spiro lifted his head and licked Nialo's olive-skinned cheek. His mate was even more beautiful than Eros. He wondered if Nialo's beauty had something to do with Morwyn's deep hatred. He turned his attention to Nialo's cock. It was even more perfect than Nialo's face and body.

"Come. Let's find Neo and the others." Nialo got to his feet and opened Spiro's wardrobe. "I'll have to find something to wear, but this will do for now." He withdrew one of Spiro's shear white shifts and tied it around his waist. The result was stunning.

Spiro took several tentative steps towards Nialo. His paws led him to believe he was some sort of cat, but he moved like a lumbering cow. He stopped to look at himself in the mirror and was surprised to see a giant white tiger.

"You're magnificent," Nialo whispered.

Although the beast in the mirror was gorgeous, Spiro had a hard time reconciling that the reflexion was his own. He turned away from the mirror and joined Nialo. Looking up at his mate, he wondered if his feelings were unique. *Is this the reason you forgot you were Nialo? Was it easier that way?* Spiro roared in frustration at the inability to speak.

Nialo gripped Spiro by the scruff. The touch immediately served to calm Spiro's anxiety. "Let's go."

* * * *

Within moments of leaving the privacy of Spiro's room, a guard stepped in front of Nialo. "Halt," the guard ordered.

Nialo held up his hands. "I am Nialo, and this is Spiro," he declared, inclining his head towards the white tiger. "We need to speak to Neo."

The guard continued to stare at Nialo until he became uncomfortable.

"Can we pass?" Nialo asked. He didn't dare reach out to the man for fear of what would happen.

Spiro diffused the situation by headbutting the guard's thigh. The man blinked several times. "I will escort you to the conference room."

"Thank you," Nialo replied.

When the guard started to reach for Nialo, Nialo quickly took a step back. "No. To touch me is to die."

"Tough guy, huh?" the guard asked.

"Morwyn is my twin if that tells you anything." Nialo hated to scare the guard, but it was imperative that he made people understand the consequences of their actions.

The guard's eyes went wide. Obviously, he'd heard the tales of Morwyn. "Very well."

Nialo unconsciously rubbed his chest. It hurt that the guard didn't recognise his name. Had he been forgotten? Spiro seemed to pick up on Nialo's pain because he began to rub against Nialo's legs, nearly tripping him down the stairs.

The guard kept a leery eye on the two of them. "Does Neo know you're here?" he asked.

"Yes." Nialo didn't tell the guard he and Spiro had switched places since they'd last seen Neo. It would be hard enough to explain the situation to Spiro's overprotective brother. If he tried to explain it to everyone he met, he'd have no time left to spend with the man he loved. The most important thing, and the only reason he'd agreed to Gaia's conditions, was the chance to tell Spiro all that he thought and felt. There were no guarantees that he'd make it out of Tartarus alive, and Spiro deserved to hear what he'd held silent in his heart for so long.

The guard unlocked the door to the large conference room. "I'll let Neo know you're waiting."

"You might as well contact Michael, Gunnar and Ramiro as well," Nialo said before entering the room. He stood beside the large carved table and stared down at the exotic wood grain. Everything looked strange from his new vantage point. He ran his palm over the smooth surface. "I've missed so much," he mumbled to himself.

Spiro rubbed against Nialo, offering support.

Nialo glanced down and smiled. "Thank you." He gave Spiro a rub. "Do you mind if I sit in your chair?"

Spiro licked Nialo's hand in response.

Seated, Nialo sighed. Chairs had become a lot more comfortable since he'd last sat in one. Everything felt new, different. He'd roamed the palace for hundreds of years on all fours, but it all seemed so foreign now that he stood on two legs.

Nialo suddenly felt overwhelmed. The only true moments of happiness he'd known were in his jaguar form. Fear had been his constant companion before Gaia had changed him. He was realistic. If he hadn't been able to stand up to Morwyn before, what made him think he could do it now? Clenching his fists, he let out a frustrated bellow. The room began to shake moments before the stone walls began to crumble as his fury coursed through him.

"Stop!" he heard someone scream.

It was Spiro's lapping tongue that pulled Nialo out of his destructive moment of rage. He stared into Spiro's light grey eyes as his breathing returned to normal. "Thank you."

Spiro broke eye contact and roared, drawing Nialo's attention to the door. Neo, Ramiro and Gunnar were barrelling into the conference room. Nialo quickly held up his hands. "Don't come any closer. It seems I don't yet have control of my power."

"Who are you?" Neo asked, shielding the others with his body.

"Nialo." He looked around at the devastation he'd caused. "Perhaps we should continue this outside."

Neo glanced at the white tiger at Nialo's side. "Spiro?"

"Yes," Nialo answered for his mate.

"What have you done to him?" Neo growled, taking a step towards Nialo.

"I didn't, but I can assure you, it's for his own protection." Nialo gestured to the door. "Please, let's speak outside."

Neo continued to stare at Nialo as he took a step back. "Is my brother trapped in that body?"

"No. I asked Gaia for time to say my goodbyes to Spiro before I travel to Tartarus. This was the only way I could touch him," Nialo tried to explain. "To touch me in human form would mean death."

Neo turned on his heels and gestured to the others to proceed him out of the room.

Once Nialo was left alone with Spiro, he leant down and kissed the top of his mate's head. "I'm already destroying things that I love, and I've barely started."

* * * *

Nialo sat in the lush grass with Spiro curled against his side while the others chose to sit on marble benches. "I spoke to Gaia," Nialo began. He went on to tell the others about the meeting with his mother, and the realisation that he was the only one who had a chance of defeating Morwyn.

By the time Nialo had finished, Spiro was pacing circles around him. Nialo reached out and tried his best to ease Spiro. "It's our only chance to be together," he told the big cat.

"What about King Kildare?" Ramiro asked.

"If I can find him, I'll send him back to The Realm." Nialo managed to grab the scruff on Spiro's neck and pull the white tiger towards him. He knew he needed to answer questions, but his focus was on Spiro.

"You've been in an alternate form for a long time. Will you be strong enough to defeat Morwyn?" Neo asked.

Nialo wasn't sure how to answer. His powers were most certainly intact, but killing his twin would take more than that. First, he needed to master his fear of Morwyn. "I guess we'll see."

"What happens to Morwyn if you fail?" Neo glanced from Nialo to Spiro with an apologetic smile. It was a depressing question, but one that needed to be asked.

"I'm not positive, but I believe he'll be weakened." Nialo took a deep breath. He'd given the confrontation between him and Morwyn some thought, and had decided that before he faced his twin, he needed to practice on someone else he hated. "Which is why I need to speak to Zeus before I go to Tartarus."

Neo's eyes narrowed. "Does it have anything to do with the real reason Zeus mated you to my brother?"

Nialo nodded.

"Do you think confronting him would be wise? Zeus is known for his temper," Neo reminded Nialo.

"Right now, I am more powerful than my big brother. If I succeed in killing Morwyn, my powers will be on the same level as Zeus', and I doubt I'd have the nerve to take him on." Nialo blamed Zeus almost as much as he did Morwyn for the fate he'd suffered for so long.

Spiro moved to stand in front of Nialo, blocking Nialo's view of everyone else. Nialo rubbed his face against Spiro's. "It's okay," Nialo soothed. "I'll speak with Zeus after the two of us spend time together."

Although he knew he was stronger than Zeus, Nialo wouldn't take the chance of being unable to confess his love and desire to his mate. He looked around Spiro to Neo. "I must be in Tartarus in twenty-one hours. Until then, there are a few loose ends I need to tie up."

Nialo returned his attention to Spiro. "Go back to our bedroom and wait there for me."

Spiro shook his head from side to side in protest.

"I want a few minutes alone with Neo, and I need you to respect that," Nialo pleaded.

With a huff, Spiro nuzzled his head against Nialo's chest before turning and walking away.

"Can I speak to you alone?" Nialo asked Neo.

Neo nodded before sending the others to help with the palace damage. "Is there more?" he asked once they were alone.

"I wanted the chance to thank you for rescuing me all those years ago. The years I spent in your home were the best of my life. And, I need to talk to you about Spiro, and what will happen if I'm not successful in killing Morwyn."

Neo started to reach for Nialo but pulled his hand back before it could connect. "Spiro will kill himself if you don't return."

"You can't let that happen. You'll have to make him understand that I died for the chance to hold him in my arms. Tell him I will always watch over him, no matter where I am." Nialo stopped talking and wiped the tears from his eyes. He stared at the moisture on his fingertips. It had been so long since he'd given into his sorrow.

"Gaia gave me five days to take care of Morwyn. On the sixth day, if I've failed to kill him, she will return me to The Realm, and I will forever roam the halls in jaguar form." Nialo shook his head. "I won't let that happen because it will mean the threat of my twin is still out there. I will sacrifice myself to his sword if it comes to that. I don't think Morwyn knows that our powers are amplified when we're both alive. Had Morwyn succeeded in killing me all those years ago, his power would have diminished and there would have been no reason to imprison him in Tartarus."

"Sacrificing yourself is not an option. If you fail, return to the palace. It doesn't matter to those who love you what form you're in," Neo argued.

"It does to me," Nialo whispered. "Imagine being unable to express your love to Michael. What if you were unable to kiss his lips, touch his skin or tell him how much he means to you?" Nialo wiped more tears from his cheeks. "I've already lived that torture, and I can't do it to myself or Spiro again."

Neo stared at Nialo for several moments. "I'll not tell Spiro what you're planning."

"Thank you." Nialo dipped his head to the ruler of The Realm.

Chapter Three

Still damp from his first ever shower, Nialo joined Spiro in the bedroom. He stopped at the large platter of fruit, nuts and meat the cook had prepared, and nibbled on a slice of roast beef.

"The shower is a fast way to clean, but I miss the soft, gurgling water of the spring by where I grew up." Nialo licked his fingers as he climbed onto the large satin-covered bed. Unlike Spiro, Nialo didn't bother to cover his nudity. He remembered all too well how the sight of Spiro's cock made him feel, and he wasn't about to deprive his mate.

Nialo piled several pillows against the headboard and leant back, leaving his legs splayed. "Do you have any idea how much I wanted to watch you touch yourself when our positions were reversed?"

Spiro's head rose.

Nialo wrapped his hand around his cock. "It's been so long since I've been able to do this. I know it's not easy for you to watch and not be able to participate, but I want you to remember what it looks and sounds like when I come calling your name."

Spiro sat up on his haunches and stared at Nialo's cock.

Although Nialo had laid out his plan to Neo, he didn't want Spiro to focus on anything but the two of them. He lifted his hand and spat in his palm before going back to stroke his cock. "Your body has always been perfect to me. Even when I was still deeply mired in living life as a jaguar, I used to watch you." He increased his speed and grip on the hard erection in his hand. "At the time, I couldn't reconcile my interest in your cock while I barely paid mind to Neo's, but now we both know the reason."

Nialo moaned. "I've never had a lover," he confessed. "The only hand that has ever touched me was Morwyn's. It felt wrong, dirty when he tried to handle my cock." He took a deep breath, rubbing at the wide scar on his chest. He was prepared to share with Spiro something he'd never told another living soul. "Years ago, Morwyn tried to convince me that we were meant to be together as lovers. He believed that because we were conjoined chest to chest, the Gods had blessed us with unity for a reason. I loved Morwyn because he was part of me. It would have been easy to accept him as a lover had it felt right, but I knew the first time he kissed me and touched my cock that he was wrong about the Gods' intentions. I don't think the Gods had anything at all to do with me and Morwyn being attached. I think we were meant to bring balance to the universe."

Spiro chuffed, and Nialo realised he'd stopped stroking his now flaccid cock. "Sorry, love. I'm having a hard time dealing with my memories at the moment." Nialo rolled to his side. "Come, lay beside me and let me feel your breath on my face."

Spiro settled beside Nialo.

"I will always love you," Nialo whispered, running his fingers through the soft white hair of Spiro's side. "I know this will be hard for you to understand, but I plan to ask Zeus to dissolve our mate status…"

Spiro jumped up, cutting Nialo off.

"No. Listen to me because this is very important. I will love you no matter what Zeus decides to do, but if for some reason, I don't return, I want you to be able to find love again. You won't have that choice if I die while bonded to you."

Spiro leapt from the bed and moved to sit in front of the closed door.

Nialo swung his legs over the side of the mattress and gazed down at his protective mate. "What if I ask Zeus to follow through with the dissolution only if I don't return? Would that put you at ease?"

Spiro roared in return.

"I can't die knowing you'll forever be alone. You deserve so much more than that." Nialo lowered himself to the floor. He knew nothing he could say would make Spiro feel better about the situation. He crawled to Spiro's side and collapsed against him. "Just let me hold you until it's time for my meeting with Zeus."

* * * *

Nialo entered Zeus' throne room wearing only Spiro's sheath around his waist. It was the first time since shortly after Morwyn had cut himself from Nialo that he'd laid eyes on his older brother. When he was younger, he'd thought Zeus was the most handsome man in the universe. Now, when he looked into the face of the one who had condemned not only him, but Spiro, Nialo saw only ugliness.

"I was surprised to hear you were back," Zeus began. He looked at Nialo's nearly nude body. "I see your manners have not improved over the years."

"I show respect where respect is given," Nialo replied. "I'm going to Tartarus to stand up to Morwyn once and for all, but then, that's what you've wanted all along, isn't it?"

Zeus shifted in his throne. "Why are you here?"

"To hand you an ultimatum," Nialo declared.

"How dare you," Zeus seethed, his voice deep and scratchy.

"I dare because I am more powerful and with a mere flick of my hand, I can bring this temple down around you in seconds." Nialo smiled through his hatred. "And you know that, don't you? I came to you after Morwyn separated us, and you told me to be a man and fight my own battles. You wanted the two of us to kill each other because you couldn't stand the fact that I've always been more handsome, more powerful and more loved than you."

"You don't know what you're talking about," Zeus denied.

Nialo smiled. He enjoyed having his brother on edge. It served Zeus right. For thousands of years, Zeus had cheated his way to the top and it was about time he learnt humility. "I know that you loved Neo and Spiro's mother Triana. I also know that Eros stole her from you, and that's why you condemned Spiro to a lifetime without a love." Nialo held up his hands and gestured to his body. "You had no idea I'd be back, did you, brother?"

"Tell me what you want then get out of my house!" Zeus screamed.

"Release Spiro from our mate bond if I don't return from Tartarus and give me your word that if I do return, you will never try to come between me and my family." Nialo wasn't sure Zeus would comply, but issuing the ultimatum had done a world of good for him. He felt stronger. How many years had he wanted to confront the older brother who had turned his back on him?

"I will release Spiro from the mate's bond only if he asks for it. And I will rule the way I see fit. I'm not as stupid as you seem to think, baby brother. I know that in your present form, you can't be with Spiro. You have little choice but to go to Tartarus. If you return, your powers will be insignificant to me, and I will continue to rule the way I have since taking this position from our father."

Nialo hadn't thought it possible to hate Zeus more than he already did, but he'd been wrong. Before he could control his temper, the marbled walls began to crack. He would follow through with his threat to bring the palace down. "Perhaps killing you is the warm-up I need before facing Morwyn," he said, moving towards Zeus' throne.

Zeus got to his feet. "You can try. You've already sealed Spiro's fate with me, so what do you have to lose?"

As large chunks of heavy marble began to rain down, the two brothers squared off. It was Gaia's light that filled the throne room that finally put an end to Nialo's destructive rage. "Stop. Nialo, you have a job to do," she reminded. "And, Zeus, don't forget that you can easily be replaced."

Nialo stared at his brother. "Lay a finger on Spiro, and Morwyn won't be the only one to lose his head this week."

* * * *

Nialo was sick to his stomach by the time he returned to Neo's palace. He knocked on Neo's door as he tried to figure out how to explain his actions.

Michael opened the door. "Hey."

"I need to see Neo," Nialo explained.

"He's not here. He's downstairs in the vault," Michael replied. "As you can imagine, he was upset when you left."

Nialo nodded. There were two places Neo sought solace when he was upset, the vineyard or the vault. "I'll find him."

When Nialo started to walk off, Michael stopped him. "Nialo."

Nialo turned back around. "Yes?"

"Will my father be okay?" Michael asked. Although Spiro wasn't biologically Michael's father, Spiro had raised the boy.

"I'm trying to do everything in my power to make sure of it."

"Thank you," Michael said before shutting the door.

Nialo took another calming breath. He couldn't allow his emotions to rise to the surface again. With purpose, he quickly strode to the vault. He sneered at the statue of Zeus that hid the vault's latch. The staircase slid into place and Nialo descended the steps. He found Neo seated at the long table surrounded by volumes of old texts. "I need to speak with you."

Neo pushed the book in front of him towards the centre of the table and leant back in his chair. "How'd your meeting with my father go?"

Nialo collapsed in the chair at the opposite end of the table. "I lost my temper."

"Easy to do around Zeus."

"Yes, but I'm worried that he'll take his anger out on Spiro. He's not powerful enough to take me on. It's in Zeus' nature to go against someone he knows he can overpower easily." Nialo buried his face in his hands. "I've been trying to think of somewhere to hide Spiro until I return, but there's only one place he's not welcome."

"Gaia's."

"Yes. Unfortunately, I'm not sure I trust Gaia around him either."

"What exactly did my father say?" Neo asked, his eyes narrowed.

"That Spiro's fate was sealed. Of course that came after I ruined his palace." Nialo felt like an idiot. "I didn't mean to do it. I didn't realise how much pent up hatred I had for him. Listening to him deny everything was too much, and I lost control."

"He'll have to deal with me if he harms Spiro in any way," Neo said.

"Not to hurt you, but I don't think he cares." Nialo leaned his forearms on the table. "He cast me out of his palace at a time when I had nowhere else to go. He claimed that he didn't want to get involved, but I believe he wanted Morwyn and I to destroy each other."

"Why would he want that?" Neo asked.

"Zeus was afraid that either Morwyn or I would challenge him for his throne, and he knew he wouldn't win. I'm sorry, Neo, but I don't believe family means as much to him as it should. I sometimes wonder if Gaia was trying to hide me from Morwyn or Zeus."

"So how are we going to protect Spiro?"

Nialo swallowed around the lump in his throat. He'd gone over and over the options and had only come up with one. "He'll have to go to Tartarus with me. The wards put in place in Tartarus should protect Spiro from my touch."

Neo jumped to his feet. "Absolutely not. The wards won't protect him from the blade of a sword."

"No, but hopefully, I'll have Ian's help. Morwyn will be too concerned with the threat I present to worry about two non-significants in the area."

Something sparked in Neo's eyes. Without a word, he walked over to a shelf and withdrew a large, leather bound volume. "I want to show you something."

"I don't know how to read, so it would be pointless," Nialo confessed.

Neo opened the book and sifted through several pages before turning it around to face Nialo. "It's titled War Between Good and Evil. Spiro found it years ago. We all believed it was a depiction of the war between you and Morwyn after he separated the two of you, but what if it's a war that hasn't happened yet?" He pointed to the landscape. "Does this look like the area where you fought?"

Nialo shook his head. He still remembered the freedom of flying over green rolling hills in his dragon skin. "Not at all." The picture was devoid of anything beautiful. Tall, craggy rocks against a barren landscape.

"Tell me what you see."

Nialo studied the picture. "Me and Morwyn fighting."

Neo handed Nialo a magnifying glass before tapping his finger against the bottom corner of the page. "Look closer."

Only with the aid of the magnifying glass could Nialo make out a small group of people hidden in the rocks. "White hair," he gasped.

"There are five people. I think they're supposed to be, Spiro, Ian, Ramiro, Gunnar and myself." Neo leaned over to look at the portrait again. "This war hasn't happened yet, and I think we just discovered our answer as to how we protect Spiro."

"But there's no way to tell what comes after this scene. What if Morwyn kills me and goes after the five of you? What would happen to the Blessed Creatures if something happened to you and Spiro?" Nialo couldn't imagine asking Ramiro, Gunnar and Neo to follow him in his quest to put an end to Morwyn.

Neo tapped the book again. "It's already been depicted. Whatever the outcome, it's supposed to happen."

* * * *

Once again, Nialo stood at the base of Gaia's mountain and waited for her to come to him. Much to his surprise, Ramiro had quickly agreed to accompany them to Tartarus. Although he was obviously still angry with King Ian Kildare, Ramiro was a vampire of great loyalty. Gunnar refused to let Ramiro go without him, so the two of them were busy preparing weapons and supplies. Morwyn wasn't the only powerful creature imprisoned in Tartarus. They would more than likely face beasts of children's nightmares on their journey.

"You argued with Zeus and now you're looking for me to bail you out?" Gaia's voice sounded in Nialo's head.

"No, not exactly. Zeus deserved what he got, but you know how he is. He's sworn retribution against Spiro, and I cannot allow that. I have only two options. Take Spiro to Tartarus with me, or kill both of my brothers."

Gaia was silent for several moments before speaking again. "You are stronger than you used to be. I was afraid the years in hiding would have the opposite effect."

"I'm done hiding. I have waited a long time to have the life I desire, and I'm no longer willing to let others get in my way. I will have Spiro, and I will live happily with him until the universe is no more."

Gaia made a pleased sound. "What do you want from me?"

"Will the wards in place on Tartarus protect Spiro and the others from my power?" Nialo asked.

"To an extent. As you've probably figured out, your powers are heightened when your emotions are out of control. You and Morwyn were born joined for a reason. One was meant to balance the other. It was the only reason you were given so much power."

"But I won't kill Spiro if I touch him, right?" Nialo asked again to be sure.

"Once you are both in Tartarus. He will have to travel to the underworld without you or in his alternate form to be safe," Gaia explained.

"What about the others? There are three men willing to travel with me to ensure Spiro's safety as I search for Morwyn. Will they be allowed to accompany me?"

"You know you should go through Zeus for this, but I understand why you are coming to me. If you learn nothing else, know that you cannot use your power against people and expect their respect afterwards."

"So you think I was wrong to get angry with Zeus?" Nialo asked. He found it comforting to speak to his mother after so many years of going without her wise guidance. Many people, including Zeus, were afraid of Gaia, but Nialo thought she sounded rather lonely.

"No, I think Zeus deserved whatever you gave him, but I will need to talk to him. I can't tell you the two of you will ever get along the way Neo and Spiro do, but I can promise that he will suffer my wrath if you return from ridding the world of Morwyn and Zeus is not properly grateful."

Nialo grinned. "Thank you." He brought his right arm up and clenched his fist over his heart. With a slight bow of respect, he returned to The Realm. He found Neo in the kitchen, working with one of the cooks to pack enough food and water for a week. "Need help?"

Neo glanced up. "No. I've got this handled. Ramiro and Gunnar are taking care of everything else. Why don't you go find Spiro. I know you've explained what we're doing, but he's been prowling around the grounds like he's uneasy."

Nialo left the kitchen in search of his mate. He checked the bedroom before going outside. When he still came up empty, he retreated to the kitchen. "I can't find him."

Neo rubbed his jaw. "Did you try my room? He could be in there with Michael."

"I didn't even think of that. Thanks." Nialo jogged up the steps. It wasn't until he knocked that he heard Michael's laughter. He took a step back, hating to intrude in Michael's last moments with Spiro.

Michael opened the door, his blond curls mussed to the point of wool. "Hey. Come in."

Nialo stepped into the room to find Spiro stretched out on the thick carpet, panting. "What're you two up to?"

"Wrestling," Michael answered with an excited edge to his voice.

Nialo laughed. He fondly remembered hours spent tussling with Michael in front of the fireplace at the vineyard. "I used to love to do that with you."

Michael grabbed Spiro's front paw. "I liked it, too." He rubbed the soft pads of the white tiger's foot against his cheek. "The best part is knowing I won't get my face scraped off for doing this."

"Spiro wouldn't hurt you for anything in the world," Nialo replied.

"I know." Michael turned serious. "Promise me that you won't let Morwyn harm Neo or Spiro."

Although Nialo couldn't promise they would all make it out of Tartarus alive, he could be honest. "I can give you my word that I'll die before I let something happen to either of them."

Spiro shook off Michael's hold and pounced, penning Nialo to the floor. He stood over Nialo and roared.

"He's worried about you," Michael said.

Nialo reached up and grabbed Spiro's scruff. "I know he is, and I know how frustrated his is because he can't tell me how he feels." He stared into Spiro's eyes. "But, we'll truly be together for the first time, and that means so much to me."

Spiro licked Nialo's face.

"Let me protect you," Nialo whispered.

* * * *

One moment Nialo was outside the palace and the next he was standing in a whirlwind of dirt and blowing sand. He shielded his eyes and mouth as he searched the dry landscape for some sort of windbreak. The others would be following in less than two hours, and Nialo prayed he'd have somewhere safe for Spiro to hide. He took a moment to dig a pair of sunglasses out of his backpack along with a T-shirt. The glasses in place, he tied the shirt around his head, covering his mouth and nose.

Nialo headed for one of the many rocky outcroppings in the distance. From what he could see, the entire place seemed to be void of any kind of vegetation. He wasn't sure if the wind was a constant force in the barren land, but it was Tartarus and he wouldn't take anything for granted.

With a firm grip on his pack, Nialo continued to scan the area as he trudged over the sand. He took the time to think about Morwyn. He'd been so caught up in protecting Spiro from Zeus' wrath that he hadn't thought about confronting Morwyn. Would Morwyn face Nialo or would he try to kill him in his sleep the way he'd separated them?

Pain shot through Nialo's head, sending him to his knees. As quickly as it had started, the pain vanished. He rubbed his stomach, trying to dispel the nausea that followed. Thinking back, he couldn't remember ever being sick. He'd been hurt, yes, but illness wasn't something Gods suffered from.

He looked around. It had to be Tartarus. Did it make him more human? It took several moments, but he managed to get to his feet without vomiting. What he needed was a couple of deep, cleansing breaths, but how could he breathe with the swirls of blowing sand trying to sneak their way into his mouth and nose?

Nialo eventually reached the base of the first outcropping. The rocks were sharp and rough against his skin as he ascended. It quickly became evident that the blowing sand had carved a number of deep pockets into the rock.

Confident that he'd be able to find enough shelter to shield Spiro from the worst of the blowing sand, he began to retrace his steps. When dirt blew under his glasses, Nialo lost his cool. "Stop it!" he screamed, waving his hands in front of his face.

All at once, the wind stopped completely. The individual grains of sand and dirt dropped to the ground like dead weights. Nialo removed the T-shirt from his face and took in some much needed clean air. Earlier, after the bout of nausea, he'd wrongfully assumed Tartarus had diminished his powers, but looking around, he knew that wasn't the case at all. So what was with the pain in his head?

Nialo stared down at his hands. He wished he knew where the power came from. Was it in his hands or did he do it with his mind?

"Over here," someone with a deep voice called.

Nialo spotted four silhouettes against the glaring sun. *Spiro.* Dropping his pack, he took off at a run, wishing for the first time that he had the speed of the jaguar he'd taken for granted for so many years. In the blink of an eye, he was standing in front of Spiro. "It's you," he whispered.

Spiro stared back into Nialo's eyes. "How'd you do that?"

"Do what?" Nialo asked. He wanted nothing more than to run his fingers through Spiro's long white hair, but his own fear and the expression on Spiro's face, kept him from reaching out.

Spiro pointed off into the distance. "You were there one second and in front of me the next."

Nialo didn't remember moving at such high speeds. Odd. "There's something about this place. I'm not sure where the wards are, but they don't seem to have an effect on me."

"Good. That means we're outside Morwyn's prison cell," Neo said. He looked up at the orange sky. "The sun should be lower in the sky by now."

"Look around you," Nialo replied. "Not one blade of grass, bush or tree. I doubt this place ever goes dark." He returned his attention to Spiro. With Spiro's fair skin and pale-coloured eyes, the sunlight would be brutal. It was the first time Nialo had looked upon Spiro's beauty as a man. He truly felt like the virgin he was. It didn't matter how many times he'd fantasised about making love to his mate, when he was faced with the prospect of actually touching Spiro, he was afraid. Although his body was too timid to act on his desires, Nialo's mouth was working just fine. "You're breathtaking."

"So are you," Spiro said. He took a step closer until their bodies touched. "Kiss me."

Nialo swallowed. "What if I hurt you?"

"To stand this close and not know your taste is hurting me," Spiro whispered. He tilted his head back and parted his lips.

Summoning his strength, Nialo leant down and kissed Spiro's soft lips. His eyes drifted shut as he gave Spiro the freedom to do all the tasting he wanted.

It was Neo who finally broke the spell Nialo and Spiro seemed to be under. "We'd better find shelter. Michael gave us some of his blood because we weren't sure what we'd find, but even his blood isn't enough to sustain us for long in this sunlight."

Nialo had completely forgotten about the three vampires. He pulled back and smiled at Spiro before addressing Neo. "I found a series of caves over there, but I didn't stick around long enough to see how deep they went."

Neo glanced at Spiro. "You okay?"

Spiro dropped his fingers from his lips. "Yes." He reached for his pack, but Nialo scooped it up first. "I can carry that."

Nialo grinned. "I know, but it's my first chance to really do something for you. Let me." There were so many things Nialo wanted to do, taking care of Spiro was just the start. "This way," he said, heading off towards the mountain.

Chapter Four

"Can we stop for a minute?" Spiro asked, his voice sounding breathless.

Nialo turned just in time to see his mate crumple to the ground. "Spiro!" He raced back to Spiro's side and lifted the smaller man into his arms.

Spiro opened his eyes. "I'm so tired."

Nialo got to his feet. "Hold him while I make us a shelter," he said, passing Spiro to Neo.

"How're you going to do that?" Ramiro asked.

"Just follow me." Nialo began to run up the side of the mountain. He still didn't understand where his sudden burst of power was coming from, but he knew he had to get Spiro out of the sun. Reaching a plateau about halfway to the summit, he pressed his hands against the solid rock. "I wish I had shelter to protect the man I love," he shouted to the mountain in front of him. Within moments, a hole opened up. "Bring him up here," he called down to Neo.

Nialo entered the cave, searching for anything that could harm them but found only smooth walls carved out of the stone.

"I don't know how you did this, but by the look on your face, I'd say you don't know either," Neo said, carrying Spiro inside.

Nialo dug into his backpack and withdrew a bottle of water. He walked as far back into the cave as he could and held his arms out. "Give him here."

"I can walk," Spiro answered as Neo passed him to Nialo.

"Indulge me." Nialo lowered Spiro to the rock floor. He wondered if he could bring some sand up to act as a cushion. "Now, tell me what happened down there."

"I don't know." Spiro accepted the water. "I just feel so much weaker than I usually do."

Nialo allowed Spiro several sips before pulling the water away. "It's this place. Maybe it's reacting to your fae blood." He thought of what Gaia had told him about Ian hiding from Morwyn instead of taking him on. "We need to find Ian. If you're affected, he probably is, too."

Ramiro stepped forward. "Did Gaia manage to land us anywhere near him?"

"I don't know." Nialo brushed strands of Spiro's silky white hair away from his face. "Get some sleep." He glanced over his shoulder at Ramiro. "There're more caves up and to the right. Why don't you check them out?"

Ramiro nodded and turned to leave.

"Put on your cloak," Neo reminded. "I have no idea how long Michael's blood will stay in your system here."

Ramiro grumbled. "It makes me feel like a storybook character."

"It's better than feeling like a piece of toasted marshmallow." Gunnar tossed Ramiro a hooded black cloak.

Nialo waited until Ramiro and Gunnar had left before joining Neo at the mouth of the cave. "I don't know why Spiro's reacting to Tartarus the way he is, but my powers are stronger than they've been since Morwyn and I were joined."

"Do you think it's because you're both in Tartarus?" Neo asked.

"I don't know, but I'm afraid of hurting Spiro. You saw me do this. All I did was wish for it and it happened. Same with the sandstorm I landed in the middle of." He fisted his hands. "What if I wish for something that hurts the people I love?"

"Nialo," Spiro called.

"Coming, love." Nialo held out his hand. "Would you touch me?"

"Excuse me?" Neo's eyebrows rose.

"I know I've already kissed Spiro, but after what I did to make this cave, I need to make sure I'm still okay to touch, and you're stronger than he is," Nialo explained.

Meeting Nialo's gaze, Neo held out his hand. "I'm not afraid. I don't know how it is that you can do these things, but you've always been a protector. I doubt Tartarus would change that."

Nialo held his breath and grasped Neo's hand, taking it in a firm grip. He waited, watching the skin closely for any sign of trauma. Satisfied that he wouldn't hurt Spiro, Nialo released Neo. "Thank you."

"Nialo," Spiro called again.

"Go on." Neo gave Nialo's shoulder a shove. "You two deserve a few minutes alone. I'll go see if I can help Ramiro and Gunnar find Ian."

With what felt like hundreds of butterflies in his stomach, Nialo went to Spiro. "Are you feeling better?" he asked, sitting at Spiro's side.

"I think so. Although I have no idea what happened." Spiro sat up. "Can I kiss you again?"

Despite his nerves, Nialo leant forward. "I wish you would." He accepted Spiro's tongue with enthusiasm, eager to learn. When he mimicked Spiro's actions, he was rewarded with a soft sigh. Nialo pulled back. "Did you like it?"

Spiro chuckled. "Of course." He tilted his head to the side. "What's wrong? You seem shy with me when only yesterday you were stroking your cock in front of me."

Nialo didn't know what to say. "I've always been bolder in my fantasies, but the reality is that I'm scared. I've put so much thought into holding you, that I worry about my non-existent skills."

Spiro got to his knees and pulled the white shift over his head. "You start by getting out of your clothes. You'd be amazed how naturally things will come to you after that."

With a flick of his fingers, the shift tied around Nialo's waist fell to the stone floor. He saw the subtle wince when Spiro's back hit the cold floor. "It shouldn't be this way," he mumbled. "We've waited too long."

"The important thing is being together," Spiro corrected.

Nialo stretched out beside Spiro. "We are together, but you deserve a soft bed under you."

Spiro began to laugh. "That tickles."

Nialo felt the rock under him begin to move. He grabbed Spiro and got to his feet, ready to defend the man he loved.

"It's moss," Spiro gasped, sinking to his knees.

"That's not possible." As soon as he'd said the words, he knew he sounded like a fool. The bed of moss was right there at his feet. "But I didn't wish for it," he mumbled, trying to understand.

"You said I deserved a soft bed." Spiro ran his hand over the moss. "And you gave it to me." He stretched out on his back and smiled up at Nialo.

Nialo focused on the sight before him and everything else faded away. As he fitted his nude body against Spiro's, the final pieces of who he was settled into place. He may be a God, a conjoined twin meant to rule the universe in an effort to balance good and evil, but in his heart, he was simply Spiro's mate.

"I love you," Nialo whispered before sealing his mouth over Spiro's. The kiss was soft at first, but slowly moved into an erotic dance of tongues. He found he was quite adept at kissing Spiro once he relaxed.

Spiro buried his fingers in Nialo's hair and began playfully tugging on its long strands. "Touch me," he whispered between kisses.

"I don't know where to touch first. I want to feel all of you," Nialo replied, slipping his hand between them.

"Oh, yes, right there's a good place to start." Spiro pushed against Nialo's chest. "You'll have more room if you're not on top of me."

"I'm sorry." Nialo moved to lie beside Spiro. "I didn't mean to hurt you."

Spiro put his finger to Nialo's lips. "Shhh, you didn't hurt me." He directed Nialo's hand down to his cock. "Touch me again."

With his new position, Nialo was able to fully appreciate Spiro's body. He trailed his fingers down

Spiro's chest and stomach, fascinated by the tiny bumps that formed on Spiro's skin at his touch. Spiro's body was completely hair free, something that fascinated him.

"Have you ever grown hair here?" Nialo asked, circling Spiro's cock with the tip of his finger.

"Fae don't grow body hair," Spiro answered. "Does it bother you?"

Nialo shook his head. "Just the opposite. Your body is too perfect to cover up." He wrapped his hand around Spiro's erection. "Teach me how to make love to you. What do you like?"

Spiro rolled over and tucked his legs under him. He dug into the pack he'd been using as a pillow and withdrew a small round tin. "I made this years ago in my workshop. I never understood why or how, but I've always known it was meant for my mate only."

Nialo opened the tin and took a whiff. "Flowers?"

Spiro nodded. "Flowers and other unknown ingredients. I don't actually remember creating it. One minute I was staring at your painting in the vault, and the next thing I knew, I was in my workshop scooping this into the tin."

"What's it for?" Nialo asked.

"Gather some on your fingers," Spiro instructed.

Nialo dipped his fingertips into the paste.

"Rub it on your cock. It'll ease your passage into my hole." Spiro grinned. "Don't worry. If I'm right, it should feel amazing."

Nialo stared down at his erection. Although he'd asked Spiro to teach him, he was starting to feel like a fool. He smeared the paste on his cock. Yes, he was a virgin, but he had walked in on Neo and Michael on several occasions, so he at least knew how it was done. The paste seemed to warm as soon as it made contact with his skin, making it easier to spread. Once he started to rub it on his cock, the sensations were so fantastic, it took a lot to stop. He was on the verge of coming when he said, "I can already tell that you're going to need to make some more of this."

"Noted." Spiro lifted his ass. "Now, move up behind."

"I think I know what to do from here. I've...uhh...walked in on this part before," Nialo admitted.

Spiro chuckled. "Yes, Michael told me about it the first time it happened. You'll just need to take it easy."

Easy? Nialo wasn't sure why he needed to do that, but he guessed it was because Spiro liked to make love slowly. "I can do that." He moved to kneel behind Spiro. Reaching out, he touched Spiro's alabaster skin that seemed to glow brighter in the dark depths of the cave. He trailed his hand down Spiro's back to the crease and on to the puckered skin. The paste that still clung to his fingertips seemed to ease his passage as he entered Spiro with his thumb. One glance at his erection gave him an idea. He snatched the tin off the moss blanket and gathered more paste to rub onto Spiro's hole. "Can you feel the warmth?"

Spiro moaned. "Make love to me," he whispered.

Nialo pressed two fingers against Spiro's opening and watched as they easily slid inside.

"Mmm." Spiro moved his ass from side to side. "I'm ready for you."

Nialo replaced his fingers with the crown of his cock. He closed his eyes as he pushed inside. The air left his lungs as Spiro's body sucked him deeper. He opened his eyes in surprise as warmth surged through him. Power. He could actually feel his power coursing through him with each thrust of his hips. Afraid that he was leaching power from the man he loved, he tried to pull out, but an unseen force kept his body locked with Spiro's. "Something's wrong."

Spiro glanced over his shoulder. "No. It's finally right. After all of these years of waiting, I feel complete for the first time in my life."

Nialo looked down to where he was joined with Spiro. The point of bodily contact glowed with a pale white light. "There's something happening between us."

Spiro rocked back against Nialo. "Yes, we're finally together. Don't stop, please, don't stop."

With a firm grip on Spiro's hips, Nialo closed his eyes once more. If he could use his powers to stop the wind and create a cave, he could use them to keep the most important person in the universe safe. "May you always be safe," he whispered loud enough for only his ears to hear.

Confident that his wish would protect Spiro, Nialo allowed himself to enjoy what he'd longed for. He stilled Spiro's hips. "Let me," he encouraged as he pumped his cock in and out of Spiro faster and faster until he lost himself in sensations that he'd never believed he'd experience.

Spiro cried out Nialo's name as his body tightened.

Nialo winced as pressure surrounded his cock in a vice-like grip. His body bucked as he tried to bury himself as deep as possible in Spiro's ass. "Love," he grunted as the first rope of cum shot from his cock.

"Are you both okay?" Neo shouted from the mouth of the cave.

With his body continuing to orgasm, Nialo couldn't speak. He panted in shallow breaths, hoping to get enough air into his lungs that he didn't pass out. As his vision started to get hazy, Nialo began to weaken.

"I love you," he managed to say before his world went black.

* * * *

Spiro used a ration of his water to soak one of Gunnar's T-shirts, hoping to get Nialo's body temperature down. "It's not working," he told Neo.

"It's only been a few hours. Give it time." Neo continued to pace which meant he secretly feared the worst.

Spiro continued to dab Nialo's body with the cool cloth. Although he couldn't bring himself to regret making love, he somehow knew Nialo's condition was his fault.

"Wake up. I need you." It wasn't the first time Spiro had uttered the words. After Nialo had collapsed, Spiro had cried out in surprise. Within moments, Neo and Gunnar were there to help. They rolled Nialo off Spiro and onto the bed of moss.

All at once, Nialo yawned and opened his eyes.

"You came back to me!" Spiro began to kiss every inch of Nialo's handsome face. "I was afraid I'd lost you."

One corner of Nialo's mouth twitched. "Never leaving you."

"What happened?" Spiro asked. "One minute you were fine and the next you passed out."

Nialo yawned again. "I don't know. I suddenly felt completely drained of energy."

"I have an idea why," Neo said, moving to kneel beside Nialo. "When you're ready, I need to show you something."

Spiro put his hands on Nialo's chest, trying to keep him in place. "He can look at that later. First he needs to get his strength back."

Nialo smiled up at Spiro. "I'm okay, really. I think I just needed to sleep." Despite Spiro's protests, Nialo pushed himself to a sitting position. "Did something happen? Did you find Ian?"

Neo held out his hand. "Can you stand?"

"Sure." Nialo gave Spiro a soft kiss. "I'm fine now."

Spiro had spent three hours wondering if he'd lost Nialo forever, but it seemed he was the only one still worried about Nialo's health. "Take it easy. We still don't know what made you pass out."

Nialo got to his feet. He was steady as a rock. "I seem fine. I don't know what happened, but I'd say it's over."

Not willing to let Nialo out of his sight, Spiro got to his feet and followed Nialo and Neo to the front of the cave.

"I was over on that ridge when I first spotted it. I ran back as fast as I could, sure something had happened to both of you," Neo explained.

Nialo's sharp intake of breath said it all. Spiro stared down at his bare feet that rested comfortably on a thick bed of grass. The greenery seemed to radiate from the back of the cave to the opening and down the side of the mountain. The sheer rock below them was covered in a profusion of flowering vines in all colours of the rainbow. The greenery stopped about one hundred yards down, the mountain's usual brown and red stone was a sharp contrast to the vibrant colours above it.

"How?" Nialo asked.

"I don't know, but my guess is it has something to do with you making love to Spiro." Neo squeezed

Nialo's shoulder. "As beautiful as they are, I doubt they'll last long without water."

Nialo shook his head. "I've just painted a giant bull's-eye on our location." He turned to Neo. "We need to get Spiro out of here."

"I agree, but how do we know what happened here won't happen again?" Neo asked. "Besides, Spiro didn't handle the heat well earlier. I'm worried about him going back out there so soon."

"I'm standing right here and perfectly capable of speaking for myself." Spiro crossed his arms over his chest. He didn't know what had happened to make the plants grow, but he had a strong feeling it wasn't all Nialo's doing. What he'd said to Nialo while they made love hadn't been merely words. Spiro did feel whole for the first time in his life. It was if his body had been waiting for Nialo's to fully form. As a demi-god with fae blood running through his veins, Spiro had never felt helpless when it came to dealing with nature. He'd always been able to manipulate the elements. Listening to Nialo and Neo discuss him like he was a weakling didn't set well at all. Before giving it much thought, Spiro stepped to the edge of the plateau and held out his arms. "May the skies darken and the clouds shed their tears for a land that is barren of life. Give the dirt what it wants and it will reward all who gaze upon it," he chanted.

"What're you doing, Brother?" Neo put a hand on Spiro's arm.

Spiro ignored Neo and repeated the chant. He grinned at the first clap of thunder in the distance. He stared up at the blackening sky, pleased. "Thank you, Gaia."

"You think my mother has something to do with this?" Nialo asked, pulling Spiro back towards the cave when the first raindrops started to fall.

"Of course she does." Spiro pressed his palm against Nialo's cheek. "Gaia loves nature above all else. She hides herself away from people because she doesn't understand them." He gestured to the falling rain. "Nature she understands."

"But she lives on top of a mountain devoid of any living thing other than herself," Nialo countered. Spiro could tell that Nialo wasn't arguing, he simply didn't understand.

Spiro sat down to watch the gentle but steady rainfall. "I don't claim to know Gaia's heart or soul, but I would imagine it's easier for her to surround herself with things that cannot die."

Nialo sat on the grass before gathering Spiro into his arms. "How can you know more of my mother than I do?"

"You see her as a mother, and I see her as the powerful God that she is." Spiro gave Nialo a deep kiss. "If this land turns green it will be because Gaia has wished it to be so."

Nialo stared at Spiro for several moments before speaking. "Gaia has no power in Tartarus. Whatever happened to make it rain, came from you, not her. So if this barren landscape grows lush with green foliage, it will be because you wished it to be so."

Spiro wanted to deny it, but he'd felt the vibrations in his outstretched arms when he'd said the prayer. Was it possible that the changes he'd felt in himself while making love to Nialo had manifested in his ability to control the weather? "I've never been able to do that before."

Nialo threaded his fingers through Spiro's as he stared at the rain. "I'll have to look for Morwyn soon."

Spiro tightened his grip on Nialo's hand. "Did the two of you ever get along?"

Tears filled Nialo's eyes as if he were remembering something. "Yes," he finally said. "Growing up we were best friends." He chuckled. "It wasn't easy for us to play like the other kids in the village where were raised. It was too hard to run and each time we tried, we'd fall." He shrugged. "So we spent most of our time talking...laughing. Morwyn was the first man to kiss me. He claimed he loved me, but I knew it was wrong."

Spiro had heard the story, but he refused to interrupt Nialo's memories.

"He started hiding things from me after that," Nialo said.

"How is that possible when the two of you were joined?" Spiro asked.

"Even joined, we tried to give each other moments of privacy. We had periods of quiet each day that we used for thinking or writing letters. I often drew sketches. Morwyn loved to write letters. He wouldn't tell me who he wrote to, so one day I did the unthinkable and peeked at his letter while he was writing. I never told him that I broke his trust in such a way, and I've often wondered if he'd known. Perhaps that one straying glance birthed the hatred that he now carries for me."

"Who was he writing to?" Spiro asked.

"Zeus. I didn't know who Zeus was at the time. It wasn't until after Morwyn separated us that Faelen told me Zeus was our brother. Faelen was the one who suggested I go to Zeus for help when it became apparent that Morwyn wanted me dead."

"But Zeus didn't help, did he?" Spiro's heart hurt for all that Nialo had suffered over the years.

"No. He told me that Morwyn and I had been cast out of The Realm for a reason, and I should kill Morwyn before Morwyn killed me." Nialo shook his head. "But I couldn't kill him."

"According to legend, Morwyn doesn't have a heart. They say his anger magnifies his powers and he has no remorse for the devastation he's caused. So you see, it's not that you're too weak to go up against Morwyn, it's that you have a conscience."

Nialo sprang to his feet and walked out into the rain. He stared up at the blackened sky. "I actually had the chance to kill him once. My sword was poised to slit his throat, but then he looked into my eyes and I knew the legend was wrong."

"What do you mean?" Spiro asked, joining Nialo.

"Morwyn does have a heart, at least part of one. What I saw in his eyes was sadness. You can't have that kind of pain without having a heart. The realisation shocked me, and I stumbled back." Nialo rested his chin against the top of Spiro's head. "I let him go, and soon after that Gaia turned me into Sema."

Spiro held onto Nialo as he tried to understand. He thought of the upcoming battle between Morwyn and Nialo. It was obvious that Nialo didn't want to kill Morwyn. "Let's go home. Leave Morwyn here, trapped but alive."

"The two of us cannot be together in The Realm while Morwyn still lives," Nialo replied, his voice soft, thoughtful. "I have no choice."

Before Spiro could say anything more, Nialo kissed him. "I'm going to find Ian. I'll be back soon."

Soaked, Spiro watched as Nialo started down the side of the mountain. His heart was heavy knowing Nialo would face Morwyn in battle because of him. He wandered back into the cave, bypassing the others to fall onto his bed.

"Hey, what's going on?" Neo asked, moving to sit next to Spiro.

Spiro looked up at his brother. "If you could save the life of only one person who would it be, me or Michael?"

Neo reared back. "That's a sick question."

"Yes, but one I would like an answer to." Spiro waited, already knowing the answer. Of course, Neo would choose his mate.

"I would figure out a way to save you both," Neo finally answered, surprising Spiro.

* * * *

After walking for hours, Nialo still hadn't found any sign of Ian. He'd started to believe Morwyn had killed the King of the Vampires and once Fae King. The moment he crossed the ward that kept Morwyn hostage, the rain stopped.

Nialo held his ground for several moments before stepping back outside the warded area. He may not be ready to fight his brother, but after talking about Morwyn to Spiro, he longed for a glimpse of his twin.

To Nialo's surprise, it was Ian who stepped out of a hole in the mountain overhead. No, it wasn't Ian at all, it was Faelen. Nialo doubled over as anguish shot through him. If Ian had transformed back into Faelen that could only mean Morwyn was already dead.

Nialo sank to the mud and fought the tears that threatened.

"Nialo," a soft voice called.

Shielding his eyes from the rain, Nialo looked up. Despite Gaia's punishment of Faelen, the Fae King had done his best to protect Nialo for years against Morwyn's attacks. "I'm glad to see you alive, old friend."

"What are you doing here, Nialo?" Faelen asked.

Nialo opened his mouth to answer and found he didn't have the words. He decided to redirect the conversation back to Faelen. "Gaia told me you needed help with Morwyn, but I see that she was wrong." He couldn't bring himself to congratulate Faelen.

Faelen pointed towards the sky above Nialo's head. "I take it that is your doing?"

"Spiro's," Nialo answered. He gestured for Faelen to come closer. "Come back to our cave. Neo, Ramiro and Gunnar are also there."

"Why is Neo here? Who's watching over The Realm?" Faelen asked.

"We were only given a few days to take care of Morwyn. Come back with me."

Faelen sat on a boulder and crossed his legs. "This isn't the place for Spiro, and I'm surprised you brought him here."

"I didn't have a choice. I believe Zeus would have tried to hurt Spiro if I'd left The Realm without him." Nialo knew it sounded crazy, but there was another reason he'd brought Spiro. He couldn't talk to Neo or Spiro about it, but perhaps he could talk to his old friend. "Gaia told me the only way I'd be able to touch Spiro outside of Tartarus was to kill Morwyn. I think I needed Spiro here to remind me of what I was fighting for."

"Why do you need a reminder? I thought you hated your twin."

Nialo shook his head. "I've never hated Morwyn. He hurt me, scared me and hunted me for years, but I could never bring myself to hate him even though I detest what he's done."

Faelen nodded. "I can't leave the ward without turning back into Ian. Come back tomorrow with Ramiro. I need to speak with him."

"Do you need anything?" Nialo asked, getting to his feet.

"Yes, could you ask Spiro to work his powers on this side of the ward, too?"

Right. Faelen had been in Tartarus longer than anyone had expected. No doubt his water had run out. "What about food?"

Faelen laughed. "There is no need to eat or drink here. Food is a pleasure not given to those condemned to Tartarus." He lifted his arm and took a sniff. "However, I would very much appreciate water for a bath, so if Spiro could make it rain enough to fill up one of the depressions in the rock, I would be most grateful." Faelen started back up the rock face. "Don't stray too far from your cave. The Titans are warded on the other side of the mountain from you," Faelen warned, reaching his cave.

"Thank you." Nialo started to walk off but stopped. "Wait. How do you know where our cave is?"

Faelen laughed joyfully. "Morwyn told me the second you created it. He felt it." He disappeared into the cave without another word, leaving Nialo confused.

Chapter Five

After spending an unsettling hour filling his friends in on the meeting with Faelen, Nialo led Spiro to their makeshift bed. "I wonder if the sun ever goes down here," he mumbled, stretching out with his back against the rock wall.

"Would you like it too?" Spiro asked, moulding his body against Nialo.

"Why, are you eager to try and make it happen?" Nialo stretched one arm out for Spiro to use as a pillow while he draped the other over Spiro's waist.

"Yes, but I guess that's probably the wrong thing to say." Spiro lifted his hand. "I can't explain what happened between us earlier, but my entire body tingles, like I'm supposed to be doing something with the power I feel."

Nialo kissed Spiro. "I know how that feels. With me, it's the desire to take control of situations, like with the wind earlier or the rock that was in the way of finding you sh-shelter," Nialo stumbled over the last word. What he'd taken as granted wishes had actually been his powers or a need to control. Were they the same?

Spiro rolled to his back. "The difference is you do it without asking."

Nialo stared down at his mate. "Do you think you have to ask me?"

"Don't I? You're a God—I'm just a demi-God. I'll always come second to you," Spiro explained.

Nialo wanted to argue Spiro's way of thinking, but he knew his message wouldn't get through without proof. He stood and held out his hand. "Come with me."

"What? Now? Everyone's asleep."

"That's okay." Nialo knew he had to get it right. "We can protect ourselves without them."

Spiro accepted Nialo's hand and rose.

Nialo led Spiro out of the cave. Once they were on the plateau, he helped Spiro over to a smooth rock. "Think of this as your chair." He gestured to the wet, barren landscape in the distance. "And Tartarus as your canvas." He bent and kissed Spiro's forehead. "Paint the picture."

"What do you mean?" Spiro asked.

"Whatever your body is telling you to do, do it. You want rain, make it continue, you want flowers, plant them, you want trees, raise them up." Nialo started to leave Spiro alone, but he decided to add something. "And whatever you do here, do it everywhere. I'm not sure how many souls have been condemned to Tartarus, but I have a feeling they don't all deserve to be here anymore than I deserved to be locked inside a jaguar."

Spiro looked up at Nialo. "Even if you only have half a heart, it's still bigger than anyone else's I know."

Nialo shook his head. "No, love, that honour belongs to you above all others." He kissed Spiro once more before returning to the cave.

"Is Spiro okay?" Neo asked from the darkness.

"Yes. He's painting." Nialo grinned as he sat far enough inside the cave to shield himself from Spiro while still able to keep an eye on his mate.

"Painting?"

"With his mind," Nialo replied. "Forget it. I'm watching him." He heard rustling and moments later Neo appeared at his side. "You should get some rest."

Neo leaned his back against the wall and rested his forearms on his bent knees. "Talk to me about Ian."

"Faelen," Nialo corrected. "Technically, I know they're the same person, but now that I'm back to my original form, I would prefer not to be called Sema."

"My mistake. I've never met Faelen. Once I do, I'll be able to make the distinction. Although if Faelen is suddenly friendly with Morwyn, I'm not sure I'll have anything positive to say after I meet him."

Nialo had only known Ian while he'd been in jaguar form, but he'd never liked the man. Faelen, on the other hand, had been a friend and mentor for years before they'd both been turned. "I think you'll notice the difference. The Faelen I spoke with today was the King I remembered from my childhood. I don't know if it's this place or something else, but he seems less troubled, and you're wrong about him suddenly being friends with Morwyn. They used to care a great deal for each other. If the two of them are talking again, I think that's a positive sign."

Neo watched Spiro, smiling at the way Spiro's arms were waving around. "I know a brother's love, so I can't tell you how to feel about Morwyn, but please don't trust him until he gives you a reason to."

Nialo's focus was on Neo. Even watching Spiro conduct an invisible orchestra, Neo's love for Spiro shone in his eyes. Nialo swallowed around the lump in his throat. He remembered that look. He'd seen it on Morwyn's face at unexpected moments. "I asked Zeus to make me a promise, but he never really agreed, so I need to speak to you about it."

"What's that?" Neo continued to watch Spiro.

"If something happens to me, Zeus promised he'd break the mate bond between Spiro and me…if he was asked." Nialo fisted his hands. He hated the thought of leaving Spiro.

"Why would you do that to him?" Neo asked.

"Because I love him and the thought of him going through eternity alone is unimaginable. He has so much goodness and light in him that deserves to be shared with someone special. All I'm asking is for you to make sure Zeus keeps his promise if I don't make it." The truth helped cement Nialo's decision to do whatever he had to in order to be the man Spiro spent eternity with.

"Then you'd better make sure to kick Morwyn's ass. In case you weren't aware, Zeus can't be trusted, so making him promise anything is worthless." Neo reached out before quickly pulling his hand back.

"Did you almost pet me?" Nialo asked.

"Sorry," Neo mumbled.

"Don't be. I was afraid you would think of me differently in this form. You used to always pet me when you were troubled," Nialo remembered.

"You've always been a great comfort to me." Neo looked away from Spiro. "Even now, I know that you'll protect the people I love with your life, just as you've always done."

"I feel the same way about you. That's why I trust that you'll do what's best for Spiro." Nialo rested his head against the cave wall. He'd left something out when he'd talked to all the men because he wasn't sure how Ramiro would react. "Faelen told me that Morwyn knew the moment Gaia sent me here. I don't know what's going between them, but it could have something to do with Ian returning to his Faelen form."

"Why would that make a difference? Morwyn killed Faelen's people when he went after you. I would think Faelen would want to see Morwyn dead almost as much as you do," Neo said.

Nialo bit his bottom lip. "I know what I have to do, but you're wrong about me wanting my brother dead. It weighs heavily on my heart that Morwyn has to die so I can touch the man I love."

Neo clasped Nialo's hand and squeezed. "Please don't let that big heart of yours get in the way of what needs to be done. Being able to touch Spiro is only one reason to rid the world of Morwyn. He's dangerous, Nialo. He's proven time and time again that he can't be trusted."

Nialo considered all the untruths that had been written about himself and Morwyn. How many people had confused history books for the ultimate truth over the years? "I'm not a warrior. I don't know that I can survive knowing I've taken a life," he said, confessing his greatest fear.

"What's the alternative?" Neo asked.

"That's what I need to figure out."

* * * *

Nialo woke with Spiro in his arms. He didn't remember falling asleep and had no idea what time Spiro had joined him, but the feel of his mate against him felt so incredibly right. He buried his face in Spiro's silky hair. Unbelievably, Spiro's hair still smelt of the homemade floral shampoo Spiro concocted in his workshop.

Spiro stirred. "Mmm," he groaned sleepily as he hugged Nialo. "I'm glad you're awake. I have a couple of things I need you to do for me."

Nialo grinned and reached for Spiro's cock. "Anything in particular?"

Spiro spread his legs. "I need your demolition skills, but that can wait."

Sounds of Neo, Gunnar and Ramiro waking put a stop to Nialo's exploration of Spiro's body. Unlike the previous day, the two of them were in plain sight instead of their darkened space in the back of the cave. "This will have to wait until we're alone again," Nialo whispered. He gave Spiro a deep kiss. "Show me what you need me to do."

Spiro trailed a line of kisses down Nialo's jaw and neck. "I was so excited to show you what I've done, but now I'd rather block out the others and sneak back to our bed."

"Morning," Neo greeted, ending all possibilities of further petting.

"Is it? The sun appears to be as high in the sky as it was when I went to sleep." Nialo got to his feet. "Spiro has asked for my help with a few things before I go. Tell Ramiro that as soon as I'm finished, I'll be ready to leave."

Spiro pulled Nialo towards the cave entrance. "Just keep in mind that I'm not finished," he said, excitement in his voice.

"I'm sure anything you've done will be an improvement." Nialo gasped as he stepped foot out of the cave. He glanced at Spiro. "You did this in a few hours?"

Spiro nodded. "It'll take a few days for the plants to grow and longer for the trees to mature, but I think it's a good start. I still need to figure out who created Tartarus, and how I can manipulate the lunar cycle, if there is such a thing here."

"I don't believe Tartarus is as much a place as a state of being. I think it's like The Realm. Although it's on Earth, it exists on a different plane of reality. I assume Tartarus is the same way," Nialo tried to explain.

"So who has the ability to change The Realm?" Spiro asked.

"Zeus. He may not have created it, but he is the ruler. My guess is that Gaia created The Realm, Tartarus and Earth, but by her choice, she no longer has ruling power over them." Nialo had no idea who technically ruled over Tartarus. Zeus and Cronus both used the place as a dumping ground for all who threatened their seat of power. "It might be a question that Faelen can answer."

"Does that mean you'll let me accompany you and Ramiro?" Spiro smiled up at Nialo.

"Not this time. I'm hoping Faelen will give me Morwyn's sword if he hasn't already returned it to Morwyn." Nialo stared out at the green carpeted valley below. He tried to change the subject. "Before we made love, would your powers have been great enough to do something like this?"

"Never. I've always had enough power to keep the respect of The Blessed Creatures, but a lot of what I did came from my fae blood. I've always felt somewhat short-changed in the demi-God half of who I am. Neo used to tease me that he acquired Zeus' strength while I acquired Eros' beauty." Spiro leaned against Nialo as they continued to stare at the changes in the landscape. "I still don't understand what I'm supposed to do with the new power I've been blessed with, but creating this helped stop that tingling sensation long enough for me to get some rest. The best part was how much I enjoyed bringing beauty to such a barren and inhospitable place."

"There are no set rules to how someone uses their powers. That's why those who have used them unwisely have ended up either here or dead. It's the man behind the power that matters most. Where some Gods see power as a weapon to be used against their enemies, you see it as a tool to make things better. I can't think of a wiser use."

Spiro blushed.

"Now, what would you like me to help you with?" Nialo asked.

* * * *

After creating several deep lakes at Spiro's request, Nialo travelled with Ramiro towards the warded area. He'd promised Spiro that, depending on how his meeting with Faelen went, he would bring Spiro to the warded area the following day.

"So what is going on with Spiro? Tartarus is a prison of sorts. You don't see many gardens in a normal prison let alone ones that contain the most ruthless beings in the universe." Ramiro adjusted his hood to keep the sunlight from his face.

"I think it's Spiro's way of dealing with the influx of power he's been entrusted with. It's hard to explain how uncomfortable the power is if you don't let it out on occasion. Besides, the more I think about it, the more I agree with Spiro. Those who have been condemned to Tartarus aren't going anywhere. Most are here to keep the rest of us safe, but why does that mean they have to live out their existence in a hot, dry barren land?" Nialo questioned.

"Because that's part of their punishment," Ramiro countered.

"Uranus damned his children to Tartarus on the off chance that they might decide to overthrow him. The only crime they had committed was being born. My father originally wanted Morwyn and I sent to Tartarus, but Gaia eventually convinced him that banishing us from The Realm was enough." Nialo had given the subject a lot of thought over the years. His heart bled for those sent to Tartarus who weren't criminals.

"Uranus is gone. Can't Zeus pardon his children and bring them back to The Realm?" Ramiro asked.

"Perhaps at one time he could have, but what do you suppose living in Tartarus has done to them since they were dropped here?" Nialo shook his head. "Even innocent men who are wrongfully sent to prison can become dangerous criminals by the time they're released."

Ramiro nodded in understanding. They continued their trek towards Morwyn's warded area in contemplative silence. Nialo knew it wasn't going to be easy for Ramiro to face Faelen. "I need to caution you on something before we get there," Nialo began.

"All right."

"I've already told you that Ian has returned to his Faelen form inside the ward, but I don't think you fully understand what that means."

"I assume it means my king is gone," Ramiro replied. "Just as Sema is gone."

"Yes, but even though Sema is gone, I still carry the memories of my years trapped in his form. Faelen will remember you and everything the two of you shared while he was King Kildare." Nialo stretched out his arm and stopped Ramiro from crossing the ward. "Faelen's a lot more powerful than Ian ever was, and you need to keep that in mind if you choose to confront him."

"I swore allegiance to Ian long ago, and although he's greatly disappointed me, I'm ready to speak to him," Ramiro answered.

As if on cue, Faelen stepped out of his cave. "I've been waiting for you," he greeted as he made his way down the mountain.

"He looks so different," Ramiro mumbled.

"Actually, he looks much better than he did yesterday. I assume Spiro did as asked and made it rain here so Faelen could bathe." Nialo cleared his throat. "Would you like me to leave?"

"That's up to Faelen." Ramiro's eyes narrowed as Faelen reached the bottom of the mountain and came towards them.

Nialo was on edge, not sure how Faelen or Ramiro would react to one another.

"Tell Spiro thanks for the rain," Faelen said, coming to a stop.

"I will. He'd like to do more. He claims he must see the warded area, but I won't bring him unless I can assure his safety." Nialo met Faelen's gaze. "Would you like to speak with Ramiro in private?"

Faelen's regal posture seemed to sag just a bit. "No. Ramiro isn't the only one I need to apologise to." He gestured to several nearby rocks. "Would you like to sit? This may take a while."

Nialo was the first to move towards the rocks. As he sat down, movement overhead caught his attention. He stared up at the cave in time to see someone quickly move back into the shadows. Nialo's spine straightened. "Is Morwyn up there?"

Faelen glanced up at his cave. "Yes. That's part of what I need to talk to you about."

Ramiro shot to his feet. "You've joined the enemy?"

Nialo noticed the hurt on Faelen's face before looking up to see a mirrored expression on Ramiro's. He decided to diffuse the situation. Calmly, Nialo reached out and touched Ramiro. "Sit. Let Faelen explain himself before you condemn him."

Ramiro stared incredulously at Nialo. "It doesn't bother you?"

Nialo considered his answer for several moments before speaking. "The Faelen I remember was a good man, and although I would like to assume he's still a good man, I will not make up my mind until I hear what he has to say. The past is the past. Gods and Blessed Creatures live too long to be judged solely on past actions. Wouldn't you agree?"

"I would agree that we've all done things we're not particularly proud of, but we have to live with the decisions we've made," Ramiro countered.

"I admit that I betrayed you, Ramiro," Faelen said. "As Ian, I used my position for my own selfish desires. I felt I'd been betrayed by Gaia, and decided to live for myself and no one else."

When Ramiro started to speak, Nialo pulled him down to the rock. "Let him finish," Nialo warned.

After a slight pause, Faelen continued, "As Faelen I sacrificed many of my people fighting a war I had no business in. For my loyalty to Gaia and Nialo, everything—including my people—were taken from me," he spat out in a sarcastic tone. "Did you know that Gaia considers vampires leeches? She actually called me that once. To say I was bitter would be an understatement." He leant forward and rested his forearms on his knees. "My bitterness turned to hatred when I acquired the sword Morwyn used to separate the two of you."

"Acquired it? You told me the sword had belonged to Faelen and that he gave it to you," Ramiro argued.

"I lied," Faelen confessed. "Not only did the sword not belong to me," he met Nialo's gaze, "it didn't belong to Morwyn either."

"Yes, we all know it was originally Cronus' sword," Ramiro noted.

"And that is true. So ask yourself why Cronus would banish Morwyn and Nialo and still care enough to give Morwyn the same sword he'd used to take power?" Faelen shook his head. "He didn't. Zeus took the sword from Cronus."

Nialo's heart skipped a beat. "The sword that separated me and Morwyn belonged to Zeus? How did Morwyn get it?"

"Zeus gave it to him. Well, actually, Zeus hid it under Morwyn's side of the bed," Faelen said.

"But Morwyn was the one who used it to forever separate us." Nialo refused to lay blame at Zeus' feet.

"Yes, but not for the reason you believe. Morwyn was in love with you, but you refused his advances. Seeking advice, Morwyn made the mistake of contacting Zeus for the first time. Not only did Morwyn's first letter alert Zeus that the two of you were still alive, but it gave away your location. Zeus had been warned that you and Morwyn were more powerful than he was. Once Zeus discovered your location, he set out to destroy both of you while technically keeping his own hands free of the bloodshed that would follow."

"Do you have any proof of this other than Morwyn's words?" Nialo asked.

"Yes. Although the hides are brittle from age, they are hidden in my palace. It was only after acquiring them that I knew the truth. I worked with Juniper to create his army in the hope that I could bring Morwyn back to Earth and eventually The Realm. When my plan failed, and Zeus ordered me to Tartarus with the sword, I accepted, knowing I would never return."

Although Nialo held no love for Zeus, it was hard for him to believe that Zeus could have convinced Morwyn to do what he'd done. "I will need to see the letters for myself."

"Of course," Faelen agreed.

Nialo's mind was spinning with the information. One thing was certain; he wouldn't confront Morwyn until he knew the truth. Standing, Nialo glanced at Ramiro. "You're the only one who can get me into the castle. Would you do me a favour and get directions to where these letters are stored and meet me back at the cave?"

Ramiro nodded. "It will also give me a chance to speak with Faelen."

Nialo addressed Faelen. "I will return as soon as I can verify or discount your story." It was a struggle to hold himself together as he walked away, but he would not show emotion in front of Faelen on the off chance his old friend was playing him for a fool.

* * * *

Spiro welcomed Nialo between his spread legs. "Love me," he whispered up at his mate.

"Always," Nialo said in return before kissing Spiro.

Spiro allowed Nialo to take control of the kiss, sensing that his mate needed it. Never had he seen a man so full of anguish as when Nialo had returned to the cave earlier. It had taken almost an hour to get Nialo to talk to them.

Nialo had relayed the information Faelen had given him articulately enough, but it was the turmoil in his eyes that had told the real story.

Once Ramiro had returned and notified Nialo that he had the location of the letters, Nialo had stood and retreated to the depths of the cave.

Spiro had eventually followed Nialo to their bed, but had made no move to start a conversation. Instead, he had stretched out beside Nialo and had offered his silent support.

When Nialo broke the kiss and reached for the small tin, Spiro started to roll over. "No," Nialo said, holding Spiro under him. "I need you to hold me while I make love to you."

"I'd like that," Spiro agreed.

Nialo gathered some of the paste on his fingers and smeared it across Spiro's hole. "I can't take you back to The Realm with me," Nialo said as he pressed the head of his cock to Spiro's stretched opening.

"Why?"

"I would need Gaia's help to turn you back into a tiger, but I'm not sure I trust her anymore," Nialo confessed, slowly invading Spiro's hole.

Spiro gasped, when just like their previous session, he began to feel the tingle of power thrum throughout his body. He still didn't understand where the power was coming from. At first he'd believed Nialo was transferring power to him, but he'd watched Nialo easily shatter the rocks needed to create several deep lakes in the valley below. If Nialo was sharing, how much did he have to spare without putting himself in danger?

"Do you feel it?" Nialo asked.

"Yes. Do you think that whatever's happening to me will make it possible for you to touch me in The Realm?" Spiro questioned. He wrapped his legs around Nialo's waist.

"I can't take that chance." Nialo surged deep inside before pulling out and driving in again.

As Nialo's speed and intensity increased, Spiro found it too difficult to think let alone speak. He held on and enjoyed the feel of each thrust of his mate's cock. The tingling in his body as the power moved through him only added to the sexual high Nialo's body provided. Making love with Nialo was about more than being fucked. Never again would he think of sex as a strictly physical activity. It had taken his mate to make him understand that, but it wasn't a lesson he'd forget.

Unlike their previous session, Nialo was the first to cry out his release. The surge of power Spiro received at Nialo's moment of climax pushed Spiro over the edge. He came with the same intensity he had the first time as his body continued to suck power from Nialo.

Nialo pulled out of Spiro and rolled to the side before collapsing.

Spiro brushed his hand down Nialo's face. Like before, Nialo had passed out. Spiro tried to tell himself that the transfer of power wasn't harming Nialo, but he wondered how long it could go on until it did.

Chapter Six

Although Neo returned to The Realm with Ramiro and Nialo, he decided against going to Ian's castle.

"I know this is difficult for you, but Neo's having a hard time dealing with the information as well," Ramiro told Nialo.

"I understand that. I've seen Neo work hard over the last few years to try and build a relationship with Zeus. No matter what we discover, I will always take Neo into consideration before making a decision." Nialo stood next to Ramiro outside the gates of Ian's castle. "It's warded." Nialo could feel the ward like a physical barrier.

"Yes, but I'm still in charge of the guards which means you can pass as long as you're with me." Ramiro started to reach for Nialo's arm, but quickly pulled back before his hand could touch Nialo. "Just stay close."

Nialo did as requested.

"Ian..." Ramiro shook his head. "I mean Faelen, asked me to take over for him as king, but I told him no. I've been enjoying my life with Gunnar at the vineyard. Being king is a fulltime job that holds no interest for me. I suggested a few of the more trust worthy vampires that I've dealt with over the centuries, but ultimately, it will be Neo and Spiro's decision unless Faelen returns to The Realm to hand over his crown and name a successor."

Nialo nodded as he continued to follow Ramiro up a flight of stairs and down a long hallway. He had too much on his mind to care who became the new king of the vampires.

"Here it is," Ramiro announced, unlocking Ian's bedroom door.

Nialo had never been inside the castle, but he wasn't impressed with the gilded décor and velvet furnishings. He'd much rather live at the vineyard with its comfortable Mediterranean style. He stopped in the middle of the room and stared at the empty frame above the fireplace. "That's where he kept the sword?"

"Yes," Ramiro answered as he climbed onto the massive velvet-draped bed. He ducked under the tented canopy and pressed one of the gilded angels affixed to the towering headboard. Four feet away from the bed, a large door panel slid open. "That was easy enough."

Nialo walked towards the secret doorway, allowing Ramiro to enter first. Safes of every size and make lined two walls while a large library table and single chair rested against another wall.

Ramiro stopped at the sixth safe and began to work a combination he'd obviously memorised.

"What do you think is in the rest of these?" Nialo asked.

"No idea, probably money and jewels." Ramiro opened the safe. "There are several items in this one that Faelen asked me to bring him, but he didn't mention the others." He pulled out a large black portfolio case. "This should be it. You want to check inside to make sure before we take it back to Spiro's palace?"

"No need. I can smell the old hides from here. I'd rather be safely ensconced in the vault at the palace when we look at them." Nialo waited while Ramiro filled a small bag with items from the safe. "Anything valuable that we need to get Neo's clearance on?"

Ramiro shook his head and blew out an exasperated breath. "The stuff he's asking for is all sentimental in nature, I assume, because it looks like worthless junk to me."

Nialo stepped closer, curious. "Like what?"

Ramiro held up a small wooden vase. It wasn't particularly well carved or pretty, but Ramiro had been right, it did hold sentimental value.

"Can I see that?" Nialo held out his hand and took the vase from Ramiro. "This is the one and only carving project that Morwyn and I worked on together." He ran his thumb over the amateurish gouges in the side. "We were nine and Faelen had given Morwyn a small knife that he'd come across while travelling. Morwyn wanted to keep it, but I told him we should give it to Faelen." He chuckled. "We had a huge fight, but I eventually won, like I usually did. That was probably the reason Morwyn never wanted to do another project with me." He handed the vase back to Ramiro. "What else?"

Ramiro held up a large emerald ring. "One of his rings."

Nialo shook his head. "Breasal's. Faelen's partner who died right before the war began. Faelen always believed Morwyn was behind Breasal's death. I'm surprised Faelen wants that."

Ramiro shrugged and withdrew a black lacquer box. "This one's locked, so I don't know what's inside." He placed it in the bag. "That's all he asked for."

Nialo spotted Faelen's potion box on the bottom shelf of the safe. "Would you grab that one, too? It's probably empty, but it's something every fae should have. I'll refill it from Spiro's workshop. I don't think Spiro will mind."

Ramiro retrieved the wooden box and handed it over.

"Thank you." Nialo hugged the box against him. It had been a while since he'd remembered life with Faelen before the war. Although Faelen'd had his own people to look after, he'd always made time for the unwanted conjoined twins.

* * * *

Nialo stared at the portfolio on the table. After leaving the castle, he'd gone straight to the vault while Ramiro had gone in search of Neo. Nialo thought it might be too tempting to be in the room alone with the letters, but once the door was shut behind him, he realised he may not be ready to learn the truth about what had happened.

Several minutes later, the door opened and Michael, Neo and Ramiro walked into the room. Ramiro stopped long enough to close and bolt the door for added privacy. Although the vault was off limits to all but a select few, they couldn't take any chances with the material they were about to dissect.

Michael turned on a dim lamp that sat in the middle of the table before setting a box of cotton gloves out and turning off the overhead light.

Nialo grinned, remembering the young man with the mop of blond curls who had shown up at the vineyard. Little did any of them know, Michael would be the one to pull Neo out of his self-exiled existence. For that alone, Michael had won a place in Nialo's heart forever, but Michael had gone above and beyond by treating Sema like a member of the family.

"What?" Michael asked when he noticed Nialo staring at him.

Nialo shrugged. It wasn't the time to get sentimental. "Just wondering when you were going to get a haircut."

"Never," Neo said, answering for Michael. "His mate happens to like it."

Nialo rolled his eyes. He decided he'd put the letters off long enough. "Should we open that?" he asked, gesturing to the portfolio.

"Go ahead," Neo encouraged.

Nialo sat back in his chair and crossed his arms. "I'd rather not."

Michael unzipped the folder and spread it out. The portfolio contained a small stack of thin animal hides with ancient Greek lettering. Michael looked from Neo to Nialo. "I can't read this."

Neo shook his head, indicating that he didn't want to. He didn't say whether or not he could read the ancient text, simply that he wouldn't.

Nialo's hands shook as he reached for a pair of the thin cotton gloves.

"Here," Michael said, passing Nialo some kind of tool.

"What do I do with this?" Nialo asked, putting on the gloves.

Michael moved to stand at Nialo's side. He took the instrument from Nialo's hand and used it to pinch the hide. He slid it over in front of Nialo. He then handed the pincher to Nialo and sat down without a single word being spoken.

"Thank you," Nialo said.

Michael smiled.

Nialo adjusted the light and tried to read the handwriting. It had been so long since he'd seen the ancient text that he struggled to understand it. Within a few minutes, he was so frustrated he pushed away from the table and stood. "I can't do it."

Embarrassed, Nialo unlocked the vault door and retreated to Spiro's workshop. He felt better once he was surrounded by his mate's smell. If it weren't for the fact Neo and Ramiro couldn't get back to Tartarus without him, Nialo would have immediately sought out Spiro for comfort.

Walking around the workroom, Nialo began to gather bottles of dried plants along with a few instruments that Spiro had out on the table. He had no idea what he was packing into the box, but he thought it might bring a smile to Faelen's face, so it was worth it.

After packing as many supplies into the wooden box as it would hold, Nialo stretched out on Spiro's narrow cot. He stared up at the ceiling, wondering how he'd be able to function in his male form if he couldn't even remember how to read the language he was raised on.

A knock sounded at the door, pulling Nialo out of his thoughts. "Come in."

Neo came into the room alone. "We need to talk."

Nialo sat up and swung his legs over the side of the narrow bed. "I'm sorry I left like that. I was embarrassed."

"That's okay. It was wrong of me not to be more considerate," Neo replied. "I didn't get through all of them, but I read enough to know that Zeus was using Morwyn as a means to his own gain."

"How?" Nialo asked. "That's the part I don't understand. Morwyn and I were connected. How could I not have known he was plotting with Zeus against me?"

"Morwyn was in love with you, and he wrote to ask Zeus' advice. Zeus played with Morwyn over the course of several letters, telling Morwyn that he understood and that he was sorry. There were only two damning letters. In one, Zeus told Morwyn that perhaps it was because the two of you were joined that you couldn't see him as anything but a brother. He suggested that life would be better if Morwyn took the lead and cut the bond that held the two of you together. Zeus went on to tell Morwyn he would give him a very special sword that had belonged to his father."

"Faelen was telling the truth." Numb from all that he'd heard, Nialo stood and began to pace the room. He remembered the horror of waking that morning covered in blood. He'd thought something had happened to Morwyn during the night. It wasn't until he'd looked down to discover it was his own body that was bleeding that the true horror of what had occurred had sunk in.

"I screamed for Morwyn that morning. I believed someone had taken him from me. I had no idea at the time he'd been responsible for what had happened. Faelen came to my aid, but within minutes, I'd passed out. It was almost two weeks before I opened my eyes again. During that time, Faelen had discovered Morwyn had been the one who had cut us apart. When Morwyn came to see me, I told him I hated him and to never speak to me again."

Nialo looked at Neo. "I thought he'd done it because he hated being that close to me. It broke my heart because he was the only family I had at the time."

Neo reached out and pulled Nialo into his arms. He held Nialo close for several moments before whispering, "Zeus must have sent the last letter in reply to that incident, because Zeus told Morwyn that Faelen had stolen you away from him. Zeus urged Morwyn to live up to his name and seek revenge on Faelen for pretending to love him."

Pieces began to slide in place for Nialo. "After what Morwyn did, Faelen wouldn't let me out of his sight for fear that Morwyn would try to finish the job. Faelen was afraid of what Gaia would do if he allowed Morwyn to kill me." He buried his face against Neo's neck. "So many fae died because of lies spread by Zeus."

"Zeus has gotten away with his crimes for long enough. We'll have to figure out how to deal with this."

Nialo suddenly realised what he was doing. He pulled back from Neo. "Why can I touch you?"

"I don't know," Neo replied. "I didn't even consider the consequences when I wrapped my arms around you."

"I didn't either." Nialo smiled. "I don't know what's happened, but if you can handle my touch, so can Spiro."

"Yes," Neo agreed.

A thought occurred to Nialo. "I was close to killing Morwyn once. I had him backed against a wall with a knife to his throat. Neither of us said anything, we just stared at each other. Morwyn looked at me with such love and hurt in his eyes that I couldn't do it. I dropped the knife and ran. When Gaia offered to hide me in a jaguar's form, I accepted because I felt like an animal for what I had almost done to my twin."

"What should we do about Morwyn now?" Neo asked.

"I don't know. Whether he was tricked or not, he is responsible for killing fae. I think he and I should talk and come up with a solution to our problem," Nialo said.

"And Zeus? Will you let me have a say in what happens to him?"

"Of course." Nialo wondered how much of Zeus' involvement Gaia knew about. Going up against Zeus was one thing, but taking on his mother was very different. "Can we leave for Tartarus soon?"

"Allow me to spend a few hours with Michael. I have a feeling we'll be in Tartarus for a while."

"No we won't. Gaia gave me five days to find and kill Morwyn. If I don't complete that task, which we both know I won't, she said she'd turn me back into a jaguar." Nialo sighed as the realisation of what he needed to do sank in. "I'll have to discuss this with her."

"Yes," Neo agreed. "But first, we need to be united in our decisions."

"What about Michael? Will you allow him to travel to Tartarus?" Nialo asked.

"No. He is too special to risk. Michael will stay here and watch over the Blessed Creatures."

"Then go say your goodbyes. I'll be in here when you and Ramiro are ready." Nialo laid back down on the cot and within minutes, he was sound asleep.

* * * *

"Where are they?" Spiro asked Gunnar as he continued to pace.

"They'll be here," Gunnar replied, trying to soothe Spiro.

Spiro walked out of the cave and looked around. There was nothing else to be done in the valley, but his power felt like it was about to explode out of him. "I have to do something. Take me to Morwyn's warded area."

Gunnar chuckled. "Not going to happen."

"Nialo asked me to work my powers on Morwyn's side of the wards, but I can't do that unless I at least see it. If you'll take me there, I'll stay on this side. I'm not completely crazy."

Gunnar growled and snatched up his heavy cloak. "On one condition. If you can make it cloudy without getting me all wet in the process, I'll take you."

"Deal." Spiro waited outside. He'd spent days trapped either in the cave or on the small plateau, and he couldn't wait to exert his new power for Faelen to see. He'd yet to meet the Fae King and was anxious to catch a glimpse of him.

"Let's go," Gunnar said, coming out of the cave. He started down the side of the mountain. "You have to promise to tell me if you start feeling weak like you did when we first came here."

"I will." Spiro easily followed behind Gunnar. He reached the bottom without slowing down or feeling winded.

"How're you doing?" Gunnar asked.

"Great. You?" Spiro grinned. Although the exercise felt great, it did little to alleviate the vibrating power locked inside him. He picked up his pace and soon was prodding at Gunnar's back. "Go faster."

Gunnar glanced over his shoulder. The hood was so deep Spiro could barely make out Gunnar's features. "What's your hurry?"

Spiro shook his hand. "Have you ever put air in a tire?"

"Excuse me?"

"Have you?" Spiro persisted.

"Sure," Gunnar finally answered.

"You know how there's a point when you don't know if the tire can hold any more air without exploding?"

Gunnar chuckled. "Sure."

"That's how I feel right now. I have so much excess power running through me that if I don't let it out, I feel like I'm going to pop," Spiro tried to explain.

Gunnar pointed at the sky. "Okay then, make it rain."

Spiro laughed. "Thanks for the offer, but rain comes too easily to me now. I need something bigger. I need to get to that warded area."

Gunnar held the bottom of his robe as he started to jog. "What're you going to do once you're back in The Realm? Are you planning to make daily trips to the deserts on Earth?"

"I don't know. I keep thinking that either my body will grow used to it or Nialo will stop sharing it with me each time we make love, but so far I've been wrong on both counts."

"That area over there needs some trees, I think," Gunnar said, pointing to a field of daises.

Spiro didn't really agree, but he appreciated that Gunnar was trying to understand and help. "Thanks." Without stopping, he focused his energy on visualising a cluster of five different maple trees. In the beginning, he'd had to imagine each tree individually but like the rain, the trees and plants were coming easier to him with practice. "There," he said, "those will look real pretty once they change colours."

"Don't you have to have cold weather to bring about that change? I doubt the residents of Tartarus will appreciate a winter when they don't even have clothes to cover themselves."

Spiro stared at the back of Gunnar's head. Gunnar was right, of course, but maybe that was a challenge Spiro should take on.

"Just around this bend is a big round rock that looks out onto Morwyn's warded area."

Spiro stopped when he reached the rock. He'd almost forgotten how desolate the landscape had been when they had arrived. "Wow."

"Sit up there and don't go any closer. I need to find an overhang to sit under," Gunnar informed Spiro.

"Thanks for bringing me." Spiro was used to Gunnar being an alpha wolf, he sometimes forgot that Gunnar had been turned into a vampire. "You're not too hot are you because I can make it rain if you need me to."

"I'm fine." Gunnar crammed his big body into a small space close to Spiro.

Spiro decided to do Gunnar a favour and lifted his hands to the sky. "Darkness without rain," he whispered. Heavy black clouds began to roll around in the sky.

"Thanks," Gunnar called out.

"No problem." Spiro made himself comfortable on the rock and studied the landscape beyond. He noticed a deep groove cut into the rock that ran across the warded land. Suddenly, a picture formed in his mind of a clear stream with moss-covered sides giving way to soft grass and wildflowers of all colours. As he painted the picture in his mind, his arms began to move of their own volition.

It took a little extra concentration, but he managed to make the dark clouds overhead empty rain onto Morwyn's side of the ward while keeping Gunnar dry. He worked for hours before stopping to take a break.

Trees still needed to be added along with some berry bushes. Spiro rested his chin on his knee as he analysed his work thus far. Not bad. He stood and moved to the other side of the large boulder he'd been sitting on to get a different perspective.

When he spotted Faelen bathing with another man in a shallow pool of water, Spiro couldn't look away. It wasn't Morwyn's handsome features that held Spiro's attention because Nialo was definitely the better looking of the two. It was the gentle way Morwyn's large hands splashed water onto Faelen's back.

After several moments of spying on the intimate scene, Spiro returned to his rock. He gathered his powers and tried to concentrate on adding the final items, but his mind kept going back to the sight of Faelen and Morwyn. It was obvious the two men loved each other.

"How're you doing?" Gunnar asked.

Spiro jumped in surprise. "Fine as long as you don't give me a heart attack."

Gunnar stared out at Spiro's work and whistled. "I've never heard of anyone God or demi-God who could do something so incredible so quickly." He thumped Spiro on the back. "It's beautiful."

"It will be," Spiro agreed. "It'll take a couple of days for the plants and trees to mature."

"A couple days? Damn, you're a loser," Gunnar said around a laugh.

With his energy sufficiently drained, Spiro turned to Gunnar. "I'm ready to go back. Hopefully, Nialo will be here soon."

* * * *

Nialo wasn't sure, but he believed he'd landed in almost the exact spot as when he'd arrived in Tartarus the first time. He moved away several feet and set down the heavy wooden box he'd brought for Faelen while he waited for Neo and Ramiro.

A dark hooded figure came into view carrying Spiro. Nialo took off running towards them. "What happened?"

Gunnar stopped and handed Spiro to Nialo. "I think he just overexerted himself. He damn near transformed Morwyn's area in a single sitting."

Nialo cradled Spiro in his arms as he headed for the cave. "Grab that box, would you please?"

"Sure." Gunnar glanced around. "Where're the others?"

"They'll be here. I had to go first to leave a trail for their souls to follow," Nialo explained. He reached the base of the mountain and looked down at the sleeping man in his arms. There was no way he'd be able to climb and carry Spiro. Closing his eyes, Nialo wished he and Spiro were already inside the cave.

"No fair," Nialo heard Gunnar say. He gently laid Spiro on the moss-covered bed before taking pity on

Gunnar. Nialo held out his hands and wished for the box.

"Thank you, don't worry about me, I'll get up there on my own," Gunnar called again.

Nialo grinned as he set the box down before moving to join Spiro. "You're trying to do too much," he scolded, kissing Spiro.

Spiro opened his eyes. "You're back."

"Yes, but I came back to the sight of Gunnar carrying you." Nialo pulled Spiro into his arms. "It scared me."

"I'm sorry. I need to find a balance to this whole power thing. One minute it feels like I have too much and the next I feel empty."

Nialo had a good idea of what Spiro meant. Although he no longer felt like he had too much power, he did suffer complete exhaustion after making love to Spiro. Nialo wondered how long his body would continue to transfer some of his power to Spiro. Not that he cared, really. The fact that Spiro now held some of Nialo's power allowed Nialo to touch people in The Realm, which meant he and Spiro could finally start building their lives together.

"What did you find out?" Spiro asked, his eyes fighting to stay open.

"Rest. I'll tell you later." Nialo kissed Spiro's forehead, intent on holding Spiro until he drifted into a deep sleep.

"Are you ready to talk?" Neo asked, walking into the cave.

"Spiro's asleep. If you want, you can get word to Faelen and Morwyn that we can meet them in a few hours. I want Spiro to be there with us this time, but he needs to recharge first," Nialo explained.

"I'll go. Gunnar said Spiro really did the place up right over there. I'm anxious to see it."

"I'm sure it's beautiful," Nialo answered, without releasing his hold on Spiro. "I just wish we could get his power levelled out before he really hurts himself."

"It'll come," Neo replied before leaving.

"I hope so," Nialo whispered in return.

* * * *

"Are you sure you don't want me to carry you?" Nialo asked, balancing the wooden box on one shoulder.

"I'm fine. Besides, I don't want to meet Faelen and Morwyn for the first time while being carried."

Nialo offered his arm to Spiro. "At least let me help you steady yourself." He'd thought about wishing him and Spiro to the meeting, but was afraid he'd misjudge and they'd end up inside Morwyn's ward. It wasn't that he was afraid of Morwyn anymore, but he still wasn't sure how his twin would react to Spiro.

"Are you sure you're ready for this?" Neo asked, coming up from behind Nialo.

"No, but time's running out," Nialo answered. He kept telling himself if Faelen could forgive Morwyn so could he. The years spent feeling utterly betrayed by his brother held Nialo back even though he'd told himself a million times it was wrong. He, Faelen and Morwyn were all victims of Zeus, but they hadn't managed to figure out why Zeus wanted them all dead.

According to Neo, there were only two things that Zeus cared about, fucking and power. Since Zeus was widely reputed to be a womaniser that left power.

Nialo was surprised to find seven large rocks set out in the newly-grown grass. Five were placed on one side of the ward and two on the other. He turned to Neo. "Did you cross the ward?"

"Yes. I felt it was important that we show a certain amount of trust before meeting," Neo explained. "And I refuse to sit on the ground."

"Good thinking." Nialo looked for signs of Morwyn and Faelen before setting the box down on their side of the ward. He remained standing but helped Spiro sit on the rock beside him. "Where are they?" he asked impatiently.

"They'll be here. I would imagine Morwyn's even more nervous than you are," Neo replied.

Nialo wasn't sure how that was possible. His body itched to pace the area like his jaguar had done in stressful situations, but he reminded himself that showing unease wasn't the impression he wanted to make.

Spiro reached out and clasped hands with Nialo, silently offering support. Nialo gazed down into the eyes of his mate. "I'm all right."

"Yes, you are." Spiro stared up at Nialo. "Remember, no matter what, I'll be with you."

Nialo dropped down to kneel at Spiro's side. Heedless of what others might think, he rested his head in Spiro's lap. No matter what had happened in the past, it was the future he'd yet to live.

Spiro curled his body protectively around Nialo. "Can I make a suggestion?"

Nialo nodded without looking at Spiro.

"If you were Morwyn, would you come down here? Look around you. You have the finest warriors in The Realm at your side. Yes, you're taking a risk by trusting Morwyn, but he knows what he's done to you. It seems he's the one taking the biggest risk," Spiro whispered in Nialo's ear.

Nialo took a deep breath. "What should we do? Should I send the others away?"

"No. We do need to have a meeting, but I think we need to cross the ward, just you and me. Let's meet Morwyn and Faelen where they're comfortable," Spiro offered.

Spiro was right, it would show trust, perhaps more than Nialo had. "I could go in alone, but I won't risk you."

"Risking me will prove to Morwyn that you're willing to move forward." Spiro gave Nialo a soft kiss. "Don't forget, I may not be as powerful as you are, but I'm still a demi-God and willing to follow you into the fire if that's where you lead."

"I don't deserve you," Nialo said, sitting back on his heels.

"Yes, you do." Spiro cupped Nialo's face. He glanced at Neo. "Nialo and I are going in."

"Are you crazy?" Neo asked.

"Maybe, but I'd like a closer inspection of my masterpiece, and Nialo would like to reunite with his brother without an audience." Spiro stood and took Nialo's hand. "We'll do this together."

Nialo got to his feet. "Don't follow us. We'll bring Morwyn and Faelen back once we're ready."

"I'm uneasy about this," Neo replied.

"And I would be disappointed with you if you weren't." Nialo squeezed Neo's shoulder. "It's time I stopped hiding from my brother and face him."

Nialo held his breath as he and Spiro stepped over the ward. He picked up the present he'd brought for Faelen. "Ready?"

"Yes," Spiro answered.

"Wait. You might as well take this with you," Ramiro said, passing the bag of mementos from Faelen's safe to Spiro.

As they walked towards the mountain, Nialo took a moment to appreciate Spiro's work. The power involved in creating such lush gardens out of barren rock and dirt was incredible. "This is amazing. You really out did yourself."

"Thank you. I know I need to learn how to pace myself, but I'm sure that will come with time." Spiro glanced up at Nialo. "Do you mind that my body takes some of your power when we make love?"

"Mind?" Nialo grinned. "Without your body being able to accept some of my power, I wouldn't be able to touch you in The Realm. I think there's something even more powerful than Gaia watching out for us."

They arrived at Morwyn's cave. "Hello?"

Faelen appeared. "I'm sorry. I know you've been waiting, but I can't get Morwyn to come out." He turned his attention to Spiro. "Thank you for coming."

Spiro held out the bag. "Ramiro asked me to give this to you."

"And I brought you something you didn't ask for. I raided Spiro's workshop and restocked your box." Nialo set the box on the ground in front of Faelen. He tried to peer into the cave. "Would it be okay if I went in?"

Faelen worried his bottom lip with his teeth for a moment. "Are you carrying a weapon?" he finally asked.

"No, but I know you gave Morwyn the sword, so I doubt he's in any danger from me." Nialo prayed he wasn't being set up.

Faelen shook his head. "The sword isn't here. I hid it. It was too valuable to the truth to destroy, but too painful for Morwyn to be around."

"Then there shouldn't be any problem with me going inside, right?" Nialo was so close to looking into his twin's eyes once again he could no longer suffer through small talk.

Faelen dipped his head. "I'll keep Spiro company. I have much to ask him about the plants he chose and how to keep them alive in a place like this."

Nialo gave Spiro a quick kiss and a warning. "No more creating while I'm gone."

"I doubt that I could. You haven't recharged me since you've been back." Spiro winked at Nialo. At Faelen's questioning expression, Nialo whispered in Spiro's ear. "Perhaps Faelen has an idea of how to balance your new power," he suggested.

"I'll ask," Spiro replied.

Nialo left Spiro and entered the cave. "Morwyn?"

"Stop there," a familiar voice said from the darkness.

Nialo came to a halt. "I was hoping to see you."

"Why would you want to after everything I've done?" Morwyn asked.

Nialo took another step. "Because despite everything, you're the one person who taught me how to love."

Chapter Seven

"I'm also the one who taught you betrayal," Morwyn answered from the darkness.

"No. Our mother and father taught us that lesson when we were born," Nialo argued. "I read the letters. I know Zeus was behind what you did."

Nialo heard a shuffling sound moments before Morwyn stepped into the dim light. "Zeus may have filled my head with lies, but it was my hand that hurt you." He wrapped his arms around himself. "I knew immediately that what I'd done was unforgivable, but I couldn't take it back. Those first few nights without you were the loneliest of my life. I think I went mad when you rejected me while you were recovering. You were the only one I cared about. I always believed that you would love me no matter what, but when I realised you couldn't stand the sight of me after what I'd done, I became angry, bitter."

Nialo felt Morwyn's words like a knife to the chest. "I felt the exact same way about you."

"I'm sorry. I wish I'd never reached out to Zeus for advice."

Ironically, Nialo was beginning to believe his separation from Morwyn had been divine destiny. "Do you love Faelen?"

"Yes. When he was first sent to Tartarus, I didn't trust him. He spent days sitting outside the ward begging me to talk to him, but I'd spent hundreds and hundreds of years hiding in this cave, hating myself for what I'd done. Faelen didn't give up though and eventually, he coaxed me out of my dark hiding place. He told me he'd found the letters, and that he understood why I'd done what I had." Morwyn shook his head. "He saved me from myself."

"I'm glad he did." Nialo took another step closer to Morwyn. He stared into a face identical to his own except for the scar that ran across Morwyn's chin. "I'm in love with Spiro. He's the son of Eros and a fae woman, Triana. He watches over the Blessed Creatures along with his brother, Neo." Nialo knew Neo and Morwyn would need to meet face to face, and he wanted to make sure Morwyn wasn't surprised by Neo's parentage. "Neo is Zeus' son."

Morwyn narrowed his eyes. "And you trust him?"

"Neo rescued me from a cage many years ago while I was still in my jaguar form. I lived with him until recently. Yes, I trust him with my life."

"You were in a cage? I'm sorry." Morwyn took a step towards Nialo.

"My cage was no different than yours." Nialo studied the cave Morwyn had called home for centuries. "Why haven't you made this bigger?"

"What?"

"I can't be the only one of us to have the power to change things." Nialo pressed his hand against the stone and closed his eyes. He pictured a side room that would further protect Morwyn and Faelen from the elements. His body tingled for a brief moment before he opened his eyes. A large room was carved out of the stone. "Try it," he urged.

Morwyn shook his head. "I can't. My powers left me a few days ago. I assumed it was Gaia's doing, that she was preparing me for your arrival, preparing me to die."

Spiro. Nialo stumbled back and landed on the ground.

Morwyn immediately rushed to Nialo's aid. "What happened?"

For the first time since the day Nialo had held the knife to Morwyn's throat, he was close enough to touch his twin. He reached up and brushed his fingers down Morwyn's cheek. Tears rushed down his face as he stared into eyes identical to his own.

"What's wrong?" Morwyn asked, panic in his voice.

"I think Spiro was given your powers," Nialo answered. He couldn't bring himself to tell Morwyn how good it felt to be connected to him once more.

Morwyn sat on the stone floor beside Nialo. "Will he respect them?"

Nialo smiled. "Have you seen your front yard?"

Morwyn's jaw dropped. "He did that with my power?"

"I believe so." Nialo watched Morwyn closely for any sign of distress.

"I've never tried to use my powers for something like that. I destroyed villages," Morwyn said with a strong degree of self-hatred, "and he's using the power to rebuild them," he finished in understanding. "I think it's better that Spiro has them."

Without thinking, Nialo pulled Morwyn down beside him. "Let me feel close to you," he begged. He wrapped his arms around Morwyn and the two of them clung to each other chest to chest. "I've missed you," he whispered, pushing the past aside.

Morwyn's body began to shake as he broke down in tears. "I've missed you, too."

* * * *

By the time Nialo and Morwyn emerged from the cave, hours had passed. Spiro and Faelen both jumped to their feet and rushed the two men. "Are you okay?" Spiro asked.

Nialo looked from Spiro to Morwyn then back to Spiro. "Yes. I've finally made peace with the past." He reached for Morwyn's hand. "We're both ready to discuss the future."

"Good." Spiro held out his hand. "I'm Spiro."

Morwyn stared at Spiro's hand for several heartbeats before clasping it. "Thank you for what you've done here. I'd forgotten what green looked like."

Spiro was pleased by the praise. "I've been discussing with Faelen ways to change the weather so it can continue to thrive."

"And have you come up with an answer?" Nialo asked as he led Spiro down the mountain.

"No, but we're determined to figure it out." Spiro lifted the bottom of his gown as he picked his way down the mountain. It wasn't as steep as the one he and the others were staying on, but it was higher off the ground.

Reaching the bottom, Spiro hung back enough to observe the twins. There was a lightness to Nialo's step that hadn't been there before. Spiro's heart swelled.

"It's nice to see, isn't it?" Faelen asked.

"Yes," Spiro agreed.

Reaching the ward, Spiro wasn't surprised to see that all seven rocks were now on the same side. Neo, Ramiro and Gunnar stood as they approached. Introductions were made and handshakes given before they all sat down to discuss Zeus.

"Morwyn and I have agreed that Zeus should suffer to some extent for his crimes, but not at the cost of a war," Nialo began. He turned to address Neo. "With your agreement, we would like to offer Zeus a deal. He will maintain control of Olympus, but The Realm will be taken from his control. Spiro and I will care for the Blessed Creatures in The Realm while you and Michael care for them on Earth from your home at the vineyard."

"And Morwyn?" Neo asked.

"Although misguided, Morwyn's crimes against the fae happened. To release him from Tartarus could start a civil war between the Blessed Creatures. Morwyn's agreed to remain here with Faelen." Nialo glanced at Spiro. "He no longer has his power. We believe it transferred to you."

"How is that possible?" Spiro questioned.

"After discussing it, the only thing we've been able to come up with is that it's Gaia's doing. Perhaps in order for the transfer of power to work, you and Morwyn had to be in close proximity when you and I made love for the first time. To be honest, we don't know, and we may never know. Likewise, we think that despite her protests otherwise, Gaia forced Zeus to declare you as my mate to make up for his sins against me and Morwyn."

"Just when I really start to hate Gaia, I find out she brought the two of us together." Spiro rubbed his face. "What about sending you here to kill Morwyn?"

Nialo shrugged. "Maybe she was testing my love for you. She had to know in her heart that I wouldn't be able to kill Morwyn. As much as I love you, Morwyn will always be a part of me."

Spiro looked at Neo. Although they were only half-brothers, he understood the bond that came with brotherhood. "I can accept that."

"So how do we deal with Zeus?" Neo asked.

* * * *

Nialo walked into Zeus' throne room with Neo at his side. He'd purposely left Spiro, the sword and the letters in Athena's care after presenting his case to her. Athena had agreed with Nialo's desire to stave off a war and come to a compromise. She had given him a sealed document to present to Zeus.

"Back so soon? I know you haven't killed Morwyn, I still feel his power." Zeus looked down his nose. "And what are you doing here?" he asked Neo.

"Just came to bear witness against you if needed," Neo answered smoothly.

Zeus' eyes narrowed. "What is this about?"

"I think you know." Nialo moved closer to Zeus and handed him the sealed document. "By the way, the power you feel is Spiro, not Morwyn. My mate possesses Morwyn's power, meaning as a pair, he and I can shatter Olympus, which we are prepared to do if necessary."

While Zeus cracked the seal on the parchment, Nialo continued, "I want you to know the only reason you're still alive is because Olympus needs its token figurehead. However, from this day forward, you will have no power outside of Olympus. If you try to travel to Tartarus to confront Morwyn, you will meet him man to man without your powers and you will forfeit them forever."

"You can't do that," Zeus growled, unfolding the document.

"I wouldn't bet on it, but just to be sure, we went to Athena. She is prepared to put you on trial in front of the Gods, and I dare say they won't be as kind as I'm being." Nialo stared at his older brother. "You will have no further contact with Blessed Creatures, either on Earth or in The Realm, do I make myself clear?"

Zeus stared at the parchment for several moments before crumpling it in his hands. "What about Gaia? She's not innocent in all this."

"Gaia has agreed to stay on her mountain. She has tried to clean up your messes for years, and she's finally had enough of all of it. I doubt we'll hear from her again."

With his hands curled into fists, Zeus jumped to his feet and took a step towards Nialo.

Nialo held out his hand and mimicked wrapping it around Zeus' throat. Zeus stopped abruptly and reached for the unseen hands around his neck. "I always assumed I was the gentle one in the balance of power, but it seems I was wrong." He continued to squeeze Zeus' throat. "I am the one who will do whatever's necessary to protect the people I love. This is your last warning." Nialo released Zeus and lowered his hand. "Enjoy the throne you've killed so many people for."

After one final look at Zeus, Nialo turned to Neo. "My opinions do not have to be yours. If you would like a relationship with your father, I will not condemn you or try to stand in your way."

Neo glanced at Zeus. "The only thing my father ever taught me was how to not trust people. I think I'm better off without him."

Nialo grinned at Neo. "Shall we go?"

"Yes. I think we're both finished here."

Nialo left the throne room with Neo at his side. He felt confident he'd done the right thing. He only hoped Zeus accepted his new downgraded status with dignity because although Nialo didn't want a war, he was prepared to fight one if it became necessary.

* * * *

On the walk back to the palace, Spiro stopped in front of one of the many pubs in The Realm. "Let's go inside for a celebratory drink. It'll be fun."

Nialo dug his heels in, refusing to budge when Spiro tugged on his arm. "I'm not comfortable going in there."

"Why?"

Embarrassed, Nialo felt his face heat. "I've never been inside a place like that. I won't know how to act."

Spiro leaned against Nialo. "You act like yourself. These are your people now. You have to learn to feel comfortable around them."

Nialo had never had people before, so he wasn't sure what that meant. "Will I be expected to talk to them?"

"If they talk to you first, sure. It would be rude to ignore someone." Spiro kissed Nialo's jaw. "Don't be afraid. We'll just go in for one quick drink. Maybe next week we'll work our way up to having dinner somewhere."

Still feeling uneasy, Nialo allowed Spiro to lead him into the building. It was full of Blessed Creatures, most of them weres, which made him feel more comfortable. He'd been surrounded by weres for years while living with Neo at the vineyard. Along with weres, he spotted a few vampires and a fae couple in the corner.

"How's this?" Spiro asked, stopping at a small table by the window.

"Nice." Nialo sat down. He studied the others around him, hoping to mimic their actions. "Should we have something to smoke?"

"What? No. Smoking makes your breath smell bad," Spiro admonished, handing Nialo a stiff piece of paper.

"What's this?" Nialo looked at the printed page. There were pictures along with writing.

"It's called a menu. It tells you what they serve to drink here." Spiro pointed to a picture. "Since you're new to alcohol, you might try something like that, it's a pina colada."

"Is it good?" Nialo had to admit the soft yellow drink in the picture looked rather appetising.

"If you like fruity. I prefer something stronger, but I don't think you're ready for that yet."

A tall werewoman stopped in front of their table. "It's nice to see you again," she said to Spiro.

"You, too. That's a great blouse," Spiro replied. He gestured to Nialo. "Yolanda, I'd like to introduce you to my mate, Nialo."

"Nice to meet you," Yolanda said.

Nialo glanced at Spiro before answering, "You, too. Great blouse." He hoped he got it right. He wasn't sure what a blouse was, but Spiro seemed to like it.

Yolanda looked down and plucked at her shirt. "Thank you. I just bought it." She smiled. "What can I get you two?"

"I'll have a whisky sour and…" Spiro gestured to Nialo.

"I'll try one of those potato colums."

Spiro giggled. "Pina Colada," he corrected.

"Great. Whisky sour and a pina colada coming up."

After Yolanda had left, Nialo leaned towards Spiro. "I just made myself look stupid, didn't I?"

"You were perfect." Spiro reached for Nialo's hand. "There are a lot of things you haven't experienced yet, and I can't wait to introduce them to you."

"I know how to make love," Nialo stated.

"Yes, you do, and you're quickly becoming an expert at it."

"As soon as we finish our drinks, can we go home and do it again?" With Zeus taken care of, Nialo hoped to spend many days and nights in bed with Spiro.

"Absolutely. We've got a lot of time to make up for," Spiro replied.

Yolando set down two glasses, putting the pretty yellow one in front of Nialo. "Enjoy."

Nialo stared at his drink. He didn't recognise the yellow triangle that clung to the side of the glass and pulled it off. "What's this?"

"Pineapple. It's a sweet fruit, but only eat the soft part."

Nialo lifted the fruit to his nose. "Smells good." He tested the pineapple with his teeth, making sure to only bite the soft part as Spiro had instructed. Yes. His mate was right. "It's good."

After swallowing the pineapple, he retrieved the cherry from his drink. "I know this is a cherry, but what happened to it to make it so bright?"

Spiro shrugged. "It's called a maraschino cherry, but I have no idea how it got that way. I'm sure there are men in white lab coats that figure that stuff out."

Nialo tried to hide the fact he had no idea what Spiro was talking about by plucking the cherry off its stem. He popped it into his mouth and moaned. "Oh, I like these very much."

"I think we have a jar of them at the palace. Finish your drink and we'll go check."

Nialo felt Spiro's hand move up his thigh to his groin. Yes. He wanted to go to the palace to search for some more cherries. He upended his glass and gulped the contents despite Spiro's protest.

"You're going to pay for that," Spiro teased.

Nialo opened his mouth to ask why and suddenly felt like someone had run a steel rod through his brain. He set down the glass and used his palms to apply more pressure to his exploding head, which didn't make sense, but it felt like the thing to do.

"That's called a brain freeze. It happens whenever you try to drink something that's cold too fast," Spiro explained.

"Make it stop," Nialo begged.

Spiro scooted his chair closer and draped his arms over Nialo's shoulder and kissed his cheek. "I can't do anything to help, but I can give you kisses while you suffer."

Nialo wasn't sure he liked pina coladas after all, but he did enjoy Spiro's kisses.

* * * *

"No more, I'm going to be sick," Nialo said, trying to keep his mouth closed.

Spiro rubbed the cherry against Nialo's lips. "You'd better open up or people are going to think you've been putting on lipstick."

"What's that?" Nialo asked.

Spiro seized the moment and shoved the cherry past Nialo's lips and teeth and into his mouth. "Gotcha."

Nialo chewed the cherry slowly. "Are you done now, because I really got to throw up any minute."

Spiro rolled off the bed and grabbed a hand mirror off his dresser. "Hang on, you need to see this." He pounced onto the bed and held the mirror in front of Nialo's face. "Your lips are so pretty."

With a growl, Nialo tackled Spiro, pinning his arms to the mattress. "You're going to pay for that."

"Really? And in what currency are you going to make me pay?" Spiro asked. He and Nialo had barely made it home before Nialo had tossed Spiro over a broad shoulder and carried him to their bedroom. Three hours later, Spiro had called down to the kitchen for a jar of cherries and several bottles of water. As far as Spiro was concerned, he could hide out in the bedroom forever and be perfectly content.

Adjusting his position, Nialo trapped Spiro's arms under his legs and nudged Spiro's chin with the head of his erect cock. Although uncircumcised, Nialo's cock had come out of its hiding place, ready to play. "I don't want your money."

Spiro sucked the crown into his mouth before releasing it. "You're honestly going to let me get by with a blow job? You're too easy." He licked the knob again, gathering pre-cum on his tongue.

"I'm not easy. I just like the feel of your mouth on my cock," Nialo explained.

"More than you like my ass?" Spiro questioned.

"No, but I thought I'd let your hole rest a while." Nialo directed his cock to Spiro's lips again.

"So my hole needs to rest but your cock doesn't?" Spiro used the tip of his tongue to tease the slit for several moments before giving in to the desire to feel Nialo's length in his throat.

The first time he'd swallowed Nialo's entire cock, Nialo had come without warning. Of course that had been several days earlier. Like everything Nialo did, it hadn't taken the God long to become an expert at it. Spiro particularly enjoyed the way Nialo's tongue felt as it swept over his hole.

Nialo grabbed the headboard and began fucking Spiro's throat. "That's it. Right there," he groaned.

Spiro squirmed until his hands were free of their prison. He reached up and gripped the cheeks of Nialo's ass, encouraging Nialo to thrust faster. When he brushed Nialo's virgin hole with his pinkie, he was rewarded with a shot of cum down his throat. "Mmmm," he moaned around Nialo's cock.

"Spiro," Nialo grunted as he continued to come.

Spiro concentrated on swallowing every drop of the gift Nialo was so thoughtfully providing. A few nights earlier, Nialo had questioned why Spiro's throat didn't glow the way his ass did when the two of them fucked. Spiro didn't know or care as long as he continued to get both on a regular basis. He sighed as Nialo started to soften because he knew it meant his fun was over for a few minutes.

Nialo withdrew his cock and collapsed on the bed beside Spiro. "Please don't ever get tired of doing that," he pleaded.

"No worries there. I've waited too long for you to ever turn you away, especially when it's something that involves your cock." Spiro rested his head against

Nialo's chest. As he listened to the beat of Nialo's heart, he smiled. He couldn't imagine a more perfect ending to the fairy tale that had become his life. The evil king had been locked in a dungeon called Olympus, the wronged prince finally had the love of a fae king to keep him warm and the mean ogre, Neo, had finally learnt to accept himself while finding love along the way. Spiro thought of his and Nialo's story.

Perfect. And they all lived happily ever after.

About the Author

An avid reader for years, one day Carol Lynne decided to write her own brand of erotic romance. Carol juggles between being a full-time mother and a full-time writer. These days, you can usually find Carol either cleaning jelly out of the carpet or nestled in her favourite chair writing steamy love scenes.

Carol Lynne loves to hear from readers. You can find her contact information, website details and author profile page at http://www.totallybound.com.

Totally Bound Publishing